"Tell me to stop."

Her mouth opened. He waited, praying she didn't say those words.

"Touch me," she whispered.

Joy shot through him. Before she could change her mind, he tangled one hand through her hair and tugged her towards him, kissing her hard and deep. She gasped against his mouth, then relaxed, parting her lips so he could slide his tongue inside, so he could lick and explore and drink her in.

Every muscle in his body was coiled tight. His groin throbbed, the erection straining against his zipper harder and more painful than ever. He'd been with a few women since he and Sarah had broken up, but none of them had inspired this primal reaction inside him. None of them had made his heart pound and made him hungry with desire. Sarah was the only one who did that, the only one who could satisfy his appetite, his need.

★ ★ ★

Dear Reader,

Forgiveness—so easy as a concept, but not so easy when you're the wronged party being asked for it. I'll admit, I struggle sometimes with it. It can be hard to forgive, especially when all you want to do is hold a grudge, or when you're too scared to forgive in fear that you'll be hurt again.

I decided to explore this concept with Finn and Sarah, who share a turbulent past that led to a four-year separation. As the sheriff of Serenade, Finn knows the difference between right and wrong, but the wrong he committed four years ago continues to haunt him. Asking for Sarah's forgiveness is one thing, but proving to her that he deserves it...well, that's a whole different story.

I hope you enjoy Finn and Sarah's emotional journey!

Happy reading,

Elle

ELLE KENNEDY

The Heartbreak Sheriff

ROMANTIC
SUSPENSE

Recycling programs
for this product may
not exist in your area.

ISBN-13: 978-0-373-27760-5

THE HEARTBREAK SHERIFF

www.Harlequin.com

Printed in U.S.A.

ELLE KENNEDY

A RITA® Award-nominated author, Elle Kennedy grew up in the suburbs of Toronto, Ontario, and holds a B.A. in English from York University. From an early age, she knew she wanted to be a writer, and actively began pursuing that dream when she was a teenager. She loves strong heroines and sexy alpha heroes, and just enough heat and danger to keep things interesting.

Elle loves to hear from her readers. Visit her website, www.ellekennedy.com, for the latest news or to send her a note.

To my family, for your endless support
and encouragement.

Chapter 1

"I didn't kill her."

The quiet plea pierced into Finn's heart like a dull, serrated blade, bringing a rush of pain and helplessness. He couldn't tear his eyes from the woman sitting in front of him. He'd dreamed of being in the same room as her for so long now, but not like this. Not in this tiny, airless interrogation room, with a narrow metal table separating them, those liquid-brown eyes staring at him with anguish and resentment.

"Sarah," he began, his voice coming out gruff, "just tell me what happened the night Teresa died."

Sarah Connelly gaped at him. Even with her expression awash with anger, she was still beautiful. Her thick brown hair gleamed under the fluorescent lights on the ceiling, and her mouth, though twisted in disbelief, was as lush and sensual as ever. She was the most stunning woman he'd ever seen, and the only woman who could send a shiver of desire up his spine even when she was glaring daggers at him.

"*Nothing* happened the night Teresa died," Sarah replied in a frosty voice. "I was at home, asleep. I woke up at three to give Lucy a bottle, and then I went back to bed, where I stayed until seven in the morning."

"You didn't leave the house at all?" Finn had to ask.

"No. Not until eight-thirty, when I dropped off Lucy at day care and opened the gallery."

Finn stifled a groan. "Then how did your hair and fingerprint wind up at the crime scene? Christ, Sarah, *explain* it to me!"

"Don't yell at me, Patrick." Ice slithered into her tone. "I don't know how my hair and fingerprint ended up at the scene—but I can assure you, *I wasn't there.*"

Frustration bubbled in Finn's gut. For the hundredth time, he wished Teresa Donovan had never been killed. Not because he and Teresa had been best buds or anything, but because the woman's death had brought nothing but chaos to Finn's peaceful little town.

Exactly one month ago, Teresa had been shot in the heart, her body discovered in the living room of the majestic stone mansion her ex-husband had built for her. Cole Donovan, the ex-husband, had been Finn's prime suspect, but with the help of Special Agent Jamie Crawford—who also happened to be Finn's best friend and took a leave of absence to assist him and Cole—Cole was cleared of the crime. Now Finn was back to square one, and it was definitely a position he didn't want to be in.

Especially now, with this new evidence in his possession. Evidence that pointed right at Sarah.

"Your print was on the coffee table next to the body,"

he said quietly. "Your hair was on the floor, by the puddle of blood pouring out of Teresa's chest."

Sarah's flawless fair skin went even paler. "Then someone put it there," she whispered. "I didn't kill that woman." Her voice wobbled. "I can't believe you'd even think that."

Problem was, he *didn't* think it. From the second his deputy phoned him with the news, Finn had been in a paralyzed state of doubt. Every cell in his body, every instinct in his gut, told him that Sarah wasn't a killer. He *knew* her. He'd lived with her, kissed her, held her in his arms. She had a gentle soul, an innate need to nurture everyone around her. Even picturing Sarah with a gun in her hands, sending a bullet into someone's heart, made his mind spin like a carousel.

But he was the sheriff. He'd taken an oath to protect the citizens of Serenade. And just because he hadn't been fond of Teresa Donovan—who was?—didn't mean he could overlook this new development in her murder case.

Still, that didn't stop him from murmuring, "I don't think you killed her."

The shock in Sarah's eyes was so strong it brought a spark of irritation to his gut. "What, you're surprised?" he muttered.

She spoke in an even tone. "You showed up at my place of business at eleven in the morning on a Saturday, forced me to lock up for the day, and dragged me to the police station for questioning. Was I supposed to think you were on my side?"

I'm always on your side, he wanted to say, but bit back the words. She wouldn't believe him, anyway, and really, how could he blame her? He hadn't exactly proven to her, now or in the past, that he would stick by her.

"I'm doing my job, Sarah. I couldn't ignore the evidence." He swallowed. "And I really think you shouldn't have turned down your option of having a lawyer present."

Her eyes widened. "Do I really need one?"

"You might." Reluctance clamped over him. "This doesn't look good for you. Evidence places you at the crime scene, and there are witnesses claiming you threatened the victim."

"I didn't threaten her!"

Finn sighed. "No?"

"Well, okay, maybe a little, but I didn't actually mean it," she stammered. "She provoked me."

"Tell me how."

"I already—"

"Then tell me again," he cut in. Leaning back in the uncomfortable plastic chair, he raked both hands through his hair and fixed a tired look across the table. "Please. I need to know every last detail if I'm going to make sense of this."

"Fine." Looking very prim and proper, Sarah clasped her delicate hands together. "Teresa cornered me outside the grocery store the day after I got back to town. I had Lucy with me, and Teresa made some less-than-pleasant comments about how I had to adopt a baby because no man would ever want me. She then claimed that she'd slept with you, mocked me about how I wasn't *woman enough* to hold on to you, and finished off with a lovely threat about calling social services to take Lucy away—because a mental case like me shouldn't be raising a baby."

She recited the speech in a calm, emotionless voice,

but Finn suspected the encounter had affected her more than she was letting on. He knew firsthand how cruel Teresa could be, and being taunted by that woman would have driven anyone crazy. It drove *him* crazy, just hearing that Teresa was going around town telling people she'd slept with him.

Uh-uh, no way would that have ever happened. For him to have touched that loathsome female, the sky would need to be filled with flying pigs, there'd be a skating rink down in hell, and the Easter Bunny would be coming over for Sunday breakfasts.

But that was Teresa Donovan for you. A pathological liar. A woman intent on unleashing as much pain as she could on the world.

"Two people heard you threaten her," he pointed out.

"Not my best moment," Sarah admitted. "But she was completely out of line. And it's not like I said *I'm gonna kill you, you awful shrew.*"

He winced, acutely aware of the mini-recorder whirring away on the center of the table, recording every word being uttered. *I'm gonna kill you, you awful shrew.* Good thing Finn wasn't corrupt, or an artfully edited version of that tape could've landed in court, marked Exhibit A, Connelly's confession.

"What did you say exactly?" he prompted.

"I told her if she didn't leave me and my daughter alone, she would regret it."

The threat hung in the air, an ominous black cloud that had *motive* written all over it.

"It was just talk," Sarah insisted. "Obviously I wasn't going to hurt her. I just wanted her to go away." Her face went ashen as she realized what she'd said. "Leave the grocery store," she quickly amended. "I wanted her to *walk* away. Alive. But just go somewhere else."

Silence stretched between them. Finn valiantly tried not to stare into her bottomless brown eyes, for fear that he'd get lost in them. Just being in the same room as her, just smelling the sweet fragrance of her lilac perfume was pure torture. He'd been fantasizing about this woman for four years, dreaming of holding her in his arms again, longing to see forgiveness—the forgiveness he surely didn't deserve—etched into her classically elegant features.

As far as reunions went, this was not what he'd imagined. But what choice did he have? The mayor was breathing down his neck, demanding that Finn close this case so that the citizens of Serenade could sleep easy. *Get the murderer off our streets,* Mayor Williams had snapped during their last phone conversation.

Finn agreed with Williams—he wanted to catch this killer, too.

But he knew, without a doubt, that the killer he was searching for was *not* Sarah.

"So what's going to happen now?" Sarah's soft voice pulled him back to grim reality. "I told you what happened and you're going to let me go now, right?"

Uneasiness circled his gut like a school of sharks. "I can't let you go."

Her gasp echoed in the suddenly cold air. "What do you mean, you *can't?* Am I under arrest?"

"No." Despite the lump in his throat, he had to add, "Not yet."

Incredulity flashed across her face. "I didn't do this, Finn! Someone is obviously trying to frame me."

Yep, he'd heard those words before, hadn't he? Cole Donovan had insisted the same thing, only a week ago, when the murder weapon was discovered in the town dump. Although the gun had been wiped clean of prints, Cole had been at the dump a few days after his ex-wife's murder, which had raised Finn's suspicions. But Cole's fancy big-city lawyer had made it clear to Finn that he had no case, no leg to stand on in court, and Serenade's district attorney had been inclined to agree.

The D.A., however, did not agree with Finn regarding *this* particular suspect.

"I suggested the same thing to Gregory," Finn told her, referring to Jonas Gregory, the D.A. "But he thinks the framing angle is far-fetched."

"Far-fetched?" she grumbled. "Well, it's *true*. I'm not a killer!"

"Sarah…" His voice drifted, the growing unease plaguing his body.

Her brown eyes narrowed. "What? Just spit it out, Patrick."

She only called him Patrick when she was angry with him, and right now, he didn't blame her, especially considering the bomb he was about to drop on her. "Gregory is concerned about your, ah, history of mental instability."

Silence. Sheer deafening silence, though he could swear he heard her heart thudding against the front of her royal-blue turtleneck sweater.

"I can't believe this," she finally burst out. "God, Finn, out of anyone, *you* know what I went through. Not that you cared—" her voice cracked, and so did his heart "—but you know why it happened. I battled depression, damn it! *Four* years ago! And now, what? You're going to use that to say I'm mentally ill? That I killed Teresa because I'm insane?"

"I'm not saying anything," he said hoarsely. "I'm just telling you what Gregory said."

"Well, screw Gregory!" Her entire face collapsed. "And screw you, too, Finn." A breath shuddered out of her mouth. "I think I want that lawyer now."

With a bleak nod, Finn scraped his chair back against the linoleum floor. "I'll bring you a phone."

As he exited the room and closed the door behind him, his legs shook and his chest ached as though someone had pummeled it repeatedly. Maybe not the most macho reaction, but right now, he didn't feel big and tough. He felt completely powerless.

He strode through the bull pen toward his office, ignoring the sympathetic look his deputy Anna Holt cast his way. He loved Anna to death, but right now, he didn't want the younger woman's sympathy. He just wanted to help Sarah. He couldn't stand seeing her like this.

She hadn't killed Teresa. He refused to believe that Sarah had murdered anyone, that she'd snapped under Teresa's callous taunts and taken her life.

She snapped before.

The unwelcome thought slipped into his head like a damn cat burglar. His hands instantly curled into fists and then anger and shame jolted through him. Like she'd said, he knew better than anyone why she'd broken down. And she was right, he hadn't handled it the way he should have. But the depression and post-traumatic stress she'd battled all those years ago didn't make her a killer.

Finn entered his small, cramped office and swiped the cordless phone from the cluttered desk. Before he could leave the room and let Sarah make her call, his cell phone came to life, bursting out in a ring tone that sounded like a foghorn, which his friend Jamie continued to tease him about. But, hey, it got his attention.

His jaw tightened as he glanced at the caller ID. Mayor Williams again. That man was like a damned dog with a bone, gnawing at him, refusing to let go until Finn arrested someone for Teresa's murder.

"I can't really talk now, Mayor," Finn said, his teeth aching from the forced polite tone. "I've got Connelly in custody and she requested a lawyer."

"Lawyered up, huh?" The law enforcement slang sounded absurd coming out of the mayor's mouth. "That's a sign of guilt, isn't it, Sheriff?"

"No, just a sign of intelligence," he couldn't help but reply. "She's concerned about her rights."

"Well, I'm concerned about who she might kill next. By the way, I've got Jonas Gregory here in my office. You're on speakerphone."

Finn fought a rush of annoyance. "Mayor, I don't think we should jump to conclusions. She—"

"Did she admit to threatening the victim?" Williams boomed, ignoring Finn's attempt at defusing the precarious situation.

"Yes, but—"

"Good. Then we're all set."

A spark of wariness ignited in his gut. "All set for what, Mayor?"

"Finnegan, it's Jonas," came a second male voice. "Look, I read over the reports you faxed, and I want to move forward with this. We've got trace evidence placing Connelly at the scene, she threatened the victim two months prior to her death, and she's got a history of imbalanced and reckless behavior."

Finn swallowed. "What are you saying, sir?"

"Arrest her. We've got a good enough case here, one I can take to a grand jury."

Good enough? Finn resisted the urge to hurl the

phone into the wall and watch it shatter into a hundred pieces. Sarah's life, her entire future, was in danger of being taken away for *good enough?*

"Sir, with all due respect, I think this might be premature," he said, trying to keep the desperation out of his voice. "Let me and my staff do some more investigating, make some more inquiries—"

"What more do you need?" Gregory interrupted. "Make the arrest, and then work on tying that murder weapon to Connelly. Right now, we have enough to indict."

Knowing when he was beaten, Finn's shoulders sagged, but he still made a futile attempt at getting some leniency for Sarah. "Can I let her go after she's charged? She's a single mother, and she—"

"We're not doing that woman any favors." This time it was the mayor, whose words contained a twinge of outrage that Finn would even consider such an idea. Williams spoke again, now sounding suspicious. "You're not still involved with her, are you, Sheriff?"

"Of course not, Mayor. Connelly and I ended our relationship more than four years ago."

He referred to her by her last name, hoping it would help distance himself. But it didn't. Her beautiful face was still imprinted in his mind, the memory of her soft laughter still wrapped around his heart. Didn't matter what he called her. She would always be Sarah. *His* Sarah.

"We treat her like any other criminal, Finnegan," Gregory agreed. "She stays in lockup until the bail hearing."

"And when will that be?"

"Her lawyer can petition for an emergency hearing,

but Judge Rollins is in Charleston, playing a golf tournament. I doubt he'll fly back for something so trivial."

Trivial? Finn wanted shout. Taking a mother away from her child, keeping her locked up for the weekend, was *trivial?* Rage churned in his stomach. How was a damned golf tournament more important than a woman's life?

He suddenly cursed this small town, with its one D.A. and sole judge and closed-minded attitude.

"Make the arrest and we'll meet on Monday morning at the courthouse," Gregory said, his tone brooking no argument. "We really need to figure out how she got hold of that gun."

"Yes, sir."

Finn was numb as he hung up the phone. He let it drop from his fingers, and it clattered onto the desk, knocking over a small tin of paper clips. Ignoring the mess, he simply stared into nothingness, a chill climbing up his spine.

He couldn't do this. He couldn't arrest Sarah.

This is your job.

No, it isn't, he wanted to snap, but the voice of reason was right. He was the sheriff of Serenade, North Carolina, the man elected by the townsfolk to serve and protect them.

But who would protect Sarah?

Feeling as though his legs were made of lead, he trudged back across the bull pen, ignoring the curious look Anna shot him. He made his way down the hall, pausing in front of the interrogation-room door.

Sucking in a heavy breath, he opened the door and entered the room. "Sarah," he began gruffly.

She lifted her head in confusion. "Where's the phone?"

"I can't let you make the call until after—" he exhaled in a rush "—until after you've been booked and processed."

She blinked, and then horror dawned on her achingly gorgeous face. "Finn…"

"I'm sorry, Sarah, but you're under arrest."

Chapter 2

Under arrest. Sarah couldn't wrap her head around it as she silently endured the humiliation of getting her fingerprints taken and posing for a mug shot. *A mug shot.*

How was this happening?

I'm not a killer! she wanted to scream as Anna Holt inked up the pads of the fingers on her left hand.

It wasn't Anna's fault, the woman was just doing her job, but Sarah was having trouble remembering that as the deputy gently took the impression of her thumb.

"It's procedure," Anna apologized, her dark eyes swimming with compassion. "But we do already have them on file, you know, from that Proactive Crime thing you did in high school."

And, boy, didn't she regret that decision now. For her senior-year law course, she'd done an independent study on crime prevention, with the hypothesis that if citizens were required by law to submit fingerprints and DNA, crime in an area would reduce drastically. As part of the project, she'd organized a program called Proactive Crime, which involved getting all the seniors to submit prints and saliva swabs to the police. Which meant that her information was in the Serenade department database.

And for some inconceivable reason, she'd been flagged when the Donovan evidence had been logged in.

Sarah's head continued to spin as she followed Deputy Holt down the narrow staircase leading to the basement of the station. She'd never been down here before, but she knew what she would find. They were going to put her in a cell.

Because she'd been *arrested*. For a crime she hadn't committed.

Again, how was this *happening*?

Sarah felt all the color drain from her face as she got her first glimpse of what a jail cell looked like. Seeing one in a movie didn't count. This was real. And terrifying. Her pulse raced as she stared at the long row of small cells lining the lockup area. The steel bars seemed to glare at her in accusation. The clinking of keys sounded, and she turned to see Anna unlocking one of the doors.

"You'll have to wait in here until your lawyer arrives," Anna said softly.

The metal door creaked as the deputy dragged it open. Sarah's hands trembled. The cell was maybe fifteen by fifteen, boasting a narrow cot with a thin wool blanket. That was it. No toilet. No window. Nothing but this claustrophobia-inducing little space, illuminated by a single bulb dangling from the ceiling.

"I'm sorry," Anna added.

Sucking in a shaky breath, Sarah willed up some courage and forced herself to walk into the cell, head high. She only prayed that the criminal lawyer whose name she'd picked at random from the yellow pages showed up soon.

When she was on the other side of the bars, Anna dragged the door closed, and both women flinched as she locked it into place. "The sheriff will be down soon," the young woman finished in a strained voice.

Tell him not to bother.

Sarah swallowed down the bitter retort, then watched as the deputy hurried across the cement floor in the corridor. Her footsteps faded, and then Sarah was alone.

In jail.

She sat on the cot and reached up to rub away the tears pooling in her eyes. How could anyone think she'd killed Teresa? No matter what those damn DNA results said, she *hadn't* been in Teresa's house the night she died. She'd *never* been in that woman's house.

So why did the evidence indicate she was there?

It was a question she'd been asking herself ever since Finn showed up at the gallery earlier, but so far, the answer continued to elude her. Well, not quite. The answer was actually simple: someone was framing her.

But that only raised a whole slew of new questions. First and foremost—what the *hell?*

She didn't consider herself Ms. Popularity or anything, but people in town liked her. Even after her breakdown, most of the folks stood by her, offered their support during her struggle.

Not all of them, a voice laced with hostility pointed out.

That's right. One person had no problem leaving her to face it alone.

As if his ears had been burning, Finn suddenly appeared in front of the bars. When she noticed the anguish creasing his handsome features, all she could think was *too little too late*. He could look as devastated as he wanted, act as concerned as he felt like, but she didn't need his damn support. He hadn't given it to her when it actually mattered, and she had no use for it now.

"The lawyer you called just phoned," Finn said gruffly. "He'll be here in two hours."

Two hours?

She willed away a fresh batch of tears. Okay. Two hours. She could do this.

"Thanks for letting me know," she said in a clipped voice.

She expected him to walk away, but he stayed rooted in place, studying her through the narrow bars.

"What?" she snapped.

"I just...are you okay in there?"

She gawked at him. "Are you serious? Do I *look* like I'm *okay*?"

Finn shifted, looking utterly miserable. His unmistakable turmoil did nothing to soothe her. Just being in the same room as this man brought back unwelcome memories, lingering pain that she'd tried desperately to overcome. It didn't help that he was as gorgeous as ever, with those piercing blue eyes and scruffy black hair. The broad, muscular body that used to send a thrill up her spine, the roped arms that once brought her solace.

Patrick Finnegan had been the love of her life, the only man to ever have a complete and total claim on her heart.

But then he'd gone and broken that heart. Crushed

it between his big, strong fingers, leaving her to drown in sorrow. Alone.

She hadn't thought she'd ever recover from Finn's betrayal. Hadn't thought she'd ever be able to regain the capacity to love again. But she'd survived. Let go of the trauma of the past, became strong, stable, *capable.* And now she had Lucy, the beautiful baby girl she adored, who'd changed her entire life and gave her a sense of peace and fulfillment.

Oh, God, Lucy!

"What is it, Sarah?"

She'd forgotten he was still standing there, and when she lifted her head, she saw the alarm washing across his rugged face.

"Lucy," she burst out, fear wrapping around her throat like a boa constrictor. "The day care closes at four. What time is it now?"

Finn glanced at the utility-style watch on his wrist. "One-thirty."

Her lawyer wouldn't show up for two hours, and even then, he might not be able to get her out of here in time.

"I...I need to call the center," she said, urgency lining her tone. "Maybe Maggie can take Lucy home with her when the day care closes. Or maybe..."

She trailed off, her terror amplifying. What if Maggie called social services when Sarah told her where she was? The owner of the day care might be gentle and kindhearted, but she probably wouldn't be pleased to hear that the mother of her three-month-old charge was locked up. Maggie had mentioned during their initial interview that she had a legal duty to inform child welfare if the kids under her supervision weren't being taken care of.

Sarah had only adopted Lucy three months ago, and it had been an arduous two-year process. Financially, she'd been in a good position to raise a child, what with the handsome inheritance she'd received from her aunt and the prosperous art gallery she owned and ran. But her history with depression had raised a red flag at the adoption agency. Sarah had endured dozens of home interviews, therapy sessions and surprise visits from her caseworker before finally being approved for the adoption.

But if social services were called…they would take Lucy away from her. God, she couldn't let that happen. She'd waited two long years for Lucy—she refused to have her baby snatched out of her arms, not after everything she'd gone through in order to have the chance of being a mother.

She leaped off the cot and practically launched herself at the bars, wrapping both hands around the cold steel. "You need to do something for me," she whispered.

Finn's expression darkened with suspicion. "What do you need?"

"Bring Lucy here."

He balked. "What? No way, Sarah. I can't bring a baby to lockup!"

"Please," she begged. "Please do this. If I tell Maggie what's going on, she'll have to inform social services. They'll take my baby, Finn!"

Tears spilled down her cheeks, and her hands begun to shake, vibrating against the metal bars. "Just bring her here, and then we can figure out what to do with her."

Suddenly Finn's large hands were covering her

own, his warmth seeping into her cold, white knuckles. "Sarah. *Sarah*. Calm down."

She realized her breathing had become shallow, as her head spun dizzily from the panic coursing through her blood. She was also aware that this was the first time Finn had touched her in four years, and as her heart rate slowed and she regained her senses, she yanked her hands away and pressed them to her sides.

She couldn't let him touch her. Physically, or emotionally. Just being around him sent her back to that dark place, the hole she'd fallen into after he'd abandoned her.

"The mayor would have my head if he found out I brought a baby here," Finn mumbled, averting his eyes. "I can't do it, Sarah."

"Please," she said again. "I'll call Maggie and tell her that I'm giving permission for Anna to pick up Lucy from day care. I'll say I'm tied up at work. I'll find somebody to leave her with, maybe..." A thought entered her mind. "Jamie. Jamie can take her home with her until I get out of here."

"That could work," Finn said grudgingly.

"Of course it will. You know Jamie won't say no."

He scratched his head. "Let me give her a call. I know Cole was released from the hospital today, so they should be at the cabin by now...." He removed his cell phone from the black case clipped on to his belt, edging away. "There's no service down here. I'll go upstairs to make the call."

Sarah watched him go, relief flooding her body, mingled in with the gratitude over the fact that she'd befriended Jamie Crawford. A profiler with the FBI, Jamie had come to town two weeks ago to help Finn solve Teresa's murder, and Sarah had immediately hit it off with the auburn-haired federal officer. She knew that Jamie would take care of Lucy in a heartbeat, even with Cole still recovering from the gunshot wound he'd incurred while saving Jamie from one of his ex-wife's crazed lovers.

It floored her, the madness that had enveloped Serenade after Teresa's death. Not only had Cole been a suspect, but Jamie had nearly been killed by a man who believed Cole had taken Teresa from him.

Damn that woman. Sarah had never been fond of Teresa in all the years she'd known her, and now she loathed her even more. If Teresa hadn't gotten herself killed, Sarah wouldn't be in this position right now.

But Teresa was dead, and now Sarah was framed for murder, stuck in a jail cell and separated from her child. Oh, and in close quarters with the man who'd broken her heart—might as well throw that tidbit on her growing list of Why My Life Is a Total Mess.

"Oh, my sweet girl. I'm sorry Mommy can't take you home, but I promise you, Auntie Jamie will take good care of you."

Finn's heart ached as he watched Sarah cooing to her baby, as she held the child close to her breast and planted a gentle kiss atop Lucy's head. They were in Finn's office, since he hadn't been able to stomach the thought of bringing the infant into Sarah's cell. Sarah had spoken with the day care owner and arranged for Anna to pick up the child, and she hadn't said a word to him as they'd waited, not even a thank-you.

Though he didn't particularly blame her for not expressing any gratitude toward the man who'd *arrested* her.

But now she did speak, her eyes fixed on him as she asked, "When is Jamie getting here?"

"Any minute now."

Satisfied, Sarah focused on the baby again, and Finn couldn't help but notice the resemblance between mother and child. It was odd, considering that Lucy had been adopted, yet the baby had the same almond-shaped brown eyes as Sarah, the same creamy-white skin. Watching them together was almost mesmerizing, the way Sarah's features softened as she gazed down at the baby, the way Lucy's chubby little fingers wrapped around a lock of Sarah's lustrous brown hair.

Finn forced himself to turn away, unable to fight the helpless feeling rolling around in his gut. He remembered a time when Sarah had looked at *him* with that same adoration. Before he'd broken her heart and ran as far away from her as he could, coward that he was.

But he'd grown up since then, and not a day went by that he didn't regret his decision to leave Sarah. These past two weeks had opened his mind to the grave error he'd made. Watching Jamie fall in love with Cole Donovan had made him reassess his own empty life, made him realize that the only way to fill that gaping void was to win Sarah back.

Now any possibility of doing that had been squashed. Because, really, what the hell was he supposed to say to her?

Hey, I know I just arrested you, but how about getting back together?

Not likely.

"What happens when the lawyer comes?"

Sarah's quiet voice jarred him from his thoughts.

"Can he get me out of here?" she continued, her voice quaking. "Will I be able to go home tonight?"

Pain lodged in his chest. He wanted so badly to reassure her, to tell her that she'd be holding her baby in her arms in no time, but the district attorney's words buzzed in his head like an angry hornet. "You'll need to stand in front of Judge Rollins for a bail hearing," he said carefully.

Hope brightened her face. "And he'll give me bail, right?"

"Most likely." He glanced at the baby. "You're a mother—I'm sure he'll take that into consideration when he makes his ruling. But, Sarah…"

She peered at him sharply. "But what?"

"The hearing probably won't be until Monday morning."

Her breath came out in a shocked rush. "What are you talking about?"

"Rollins is in South Carolina for some golf tournament," he admitted. "Unless your lawyer is a miracle worker, I don't think the judge is going to hurry back for a bail hearing."

The air in the small office turned as frigid as a snowy February morning. He almost winced under Sarah's cold scowl. She was looking at him as if this was his fault, like *he* was the reason the judge was off on the fairway wielding a nine iron. Before she could yell at him—which she seemed to be preparing to do—a brisk knock rapped against the door, and then Jamie Crawford poked her head inside.

"Are you okay?" Jamie asked immediately, ignoring Finn as she hurried over to Sarah.

"I'm fine, now that you're here," Sarah said, sounding relieved.

Jamie wrapped one arm around Sarah's shoulder, dwarfing the other woman with her height; at five-nine, Jamie loomed over Sarah's five-foot frame. Then she turned to Finn with a fierce look. Wonderful. Two against one, and both females seemed to blame *him* for this mess.

"What is the matter with you?" Jamie asked, disbelief dripping from her words. "You know Sarah didn't kill Teresa, Finn. I can't believe you arrested her."

"I had no choice." He resisted the urge to rip out his own hair. "You both seem to be in denial over the fact that I'm the *sheriff.* On paper, I'm not supposed to answer to anyone, but that's bull. This is politics, and the mayor and D.A. are pulling my damn strings."

"The D.A. actually thinks he's got a case?" Jamie demanded.

Finn nodded, then waited until Sarah shifted her attention to the baby before giving Jamie a pointed look. *He does have a case,* Finn communicated silently, and Jamie's lavender eyes widened slightly as she received the transmission. As a federal agent, Jamie understood law enforcement procedures, and when her expression softened, flickering with sympathy, Finn knew she understood why he'd had to arrest Sarah.

"Okay." Jamie squeezed Sarah's arm, then moved to lean against the edge of the desk. "Okay. So what's the next move? How do we get Sarah out of this?"

"All we can do is wait for the bail hearing," he said grimly. "And if this goes to trial, Sarah's attorney will build a defense for her. In the meantime, you and I will be busting our asses trying to find the real killer."

Tension hung over the room, finally broken by a tiny wail of displeasure. Finn turned his head and noticed the baby's cheeks had turned beet red. As Lucy began to cry, hiccupping between sobs, Sarah rocked her in her arms, but the gentle motions did nothing to soothe the suddenly cranky infant.

"You should take her home," Sarah whispered, glancing over at Jamie.

It was clear that the last thing Sarah wanted to do was relinquish the child, and it nearly tore out Finn's heart as he watched her hold Lucy in front of Jamie's waiting hands. The baby's cries only grew louder as she found herself in an unfamiliar pair of arms. Jamie rubbed the baby's back and murmured a few words of comfort, which only seemed to further agitate the red-faced, squirming baby.

"Go," Sarah choked out.

"Sarah—"

"Please, just go. There are diapers and bottles in the bag on Anna's desk, and if you need more formula, you can stop by my house—the spare key is under the red flowerpot beside the porch." Sarah seemed to be fighting tears. "Did you get the car seat?"

"Yeah, I stopped by the gallery like Finn asked and took it from your car."

"Then you're all set." Sarah gave a bright smile that didn't quite reach her eyes.

"Sarah...I'll take good care of her," Jamie murmured. "I promise."

"I know."

As Lucy continued to wail, Sarah moved closer to brush her lips over the baby's forehead. "Be good for Jamie," she said softly.

Holding the crying infant, Jamie walked to the door, pausing only to shoot Finn a look that said, *Fix this. Now.* She left the office, and they could hear her footsteps in the bull pen. Lucy's distressed cries grew muffled and then eventually faded as Jamie left the station with the baby.

Sarah stared at the door for an impossibly long time, before finally turning to Finn.

His stomach clenched at her lifeless expression. She looked as though someone had ripped the one thing she cared about right out of her arms, which, in fact, was what had just happened.

"Sweetheart," he started, the old endearment slipping from his mouth before he could stop it.

The dull shine to her eyes exploded into a smoldering burst of anger. "Don't you *dare* call me that."

The vehemence in her voice had him stepping back, stricken.

"And don't you dare pretend you're going to help me get out of this," she continued, her cheeks flushed with fury. "*You* got me into this. I don't care what the evidence says, or what the D.A. thinks, you know I didn't kill anyone!"

"And I'm going to help you prove that," he said hoarsely.

"Don't bother," she snapped. "You've already proven that you're incapable of standing by me when things get a little too tough for your liking. So, frankly, I don't want or need your help, Patrick." She was breathing heavily now. "Now take me back to my cell."

"Damn it, Sarah—"

"Take me. Back. To my cell."

Chapter 3

Sarah woke up the next morning feeling downright disoriented. When she stuck out her arm to fumble for the alarm clock, she felt nothing but cold air. When she instinctively turned to the right to glance over at Lucy's crib, she found herself staring at a cement wall.

She shot up into a sitting position, shoving strands of hair from her eyes as she realized she wasn't in her cozy bedroom—she was in a jail cell.

She still wore the turtleneck and jeans she'd had on yesterday, which she'd opted to sleep in because the alternative had been too humiliating to accept. The light blue prison-issued jumpsuit was still where she'd left it—on the floor next to the metal bars. The very thought of putting on that garment had brought a wave of nausea to her belly. She might be stuck in jail, but no way would she allow Finn and his deputies to dress her up like a common criminal.

Yesterday's meeting with her new lawyer, Daniel Chin, had been a total disappointment. The mild-mannered Korean man had been unable to get in touch with the judge and, in a rueful voice, he'd told her that she had no choice but to spend the weekend in lockup. After he left, Anna had taken her back to her cell. Dinner had consisted of sandwiches from the town deli, a luxury she doubted other prisoners got to experience. She'd fallen asleep at ten, though she'd spent most of the night tossing and turning on the thin, uncomfortable cot.

Rubbing her tired eyes, she rose to her feet and stretched her legs, wondering when someone would come down to take her to the washroom. Just as she thought it, a door creaked open, and then Finn strode up to the cell.

He looked exhausted, his blue eyes lined with red, and she noticed his clothes were rumpled, as if he'd slept in them. "Anna will be down in a second to take you to wash up," he started roughly. "But first I wanted a moment alone with you."

Her heart did an unwitting flip. She knew she wasn't allowed to feel anything for this man, but there was just something about him this morning that brought a rush of warmth to her stomach. Maybe it was the messy hair, or the hard glint in his eyes. He might be polite and pleasant when he was on duty, but Sarah had known him before he'd been elected sheriff, back when he'd had the whole bad-boy thing going on.

She still remembered the day they'd bumped into each other at the lake. Finn had been a few years ahead of her in high school, but their paths had never crossed until that day. She'd been twenty-two, just back from college, and she'd been walking along the lakeshore, debating if she should use part of her inheritance to buy the art gallery that had recently come up for sale in town. So lost in thought, she hadn't noticed Finn until she'd stumbled right into his hard, muscular chest. The attraction between them had been fast, primal. For a good girl like her, the pull of desire toward the rough and sensual deputy had been disconcerting. And Finn hadn't been so diplomatic back then. He spoke what was on his mind, no matter how crude, and his bold, sexy words had thrilled her. She'd fallen head over heels for him, captivated by his gruff nature and magnetic sexuality, even though she knew her feelings for him were too damn dangerous.

She caught a glimpse of that rough edge now, and those old feelings of desire rippled through her.

Ignoring her body's traitorous reaction, she met Finn's gaze and said, "Do we have to do this first thing in the morning? I just woke up."

"And I never went to sleep," he muttered back. "I was in the chair in my office all night, trying to figure out how to say this, so—"

She wrinkled her brow. "You slept in your office?"

He glanced at her as if he couldn't believe she'd even ask. "You honestly thought I could go home and get into my big comfortable bed knowing that you were spending the night in a cell? Jesus, Sarah."

Her heart lurched again. Lord, why wouldn't it quit doing that? And why did the image of Finn squished in his desk chair, as he sat awake all night, make her pulse speed up?

"Anyway, I did some thinking," he went on, awkwardly resting his hands on the bars, "and I realized the direct approach is the way to go." Frowning, he held her gaze. "I *am* going to help you, Sarah, no matter how many times you tell me you don't need my help. Because you know what? I don't give a damn what you say—you *do* need me. And you have me, whether you like it or not."

She arched both eyebrows. "You haven't changed at all, have you? Still get off on ordering people around."

A ferocious expression darkened his face. "I *have* changed. I've changed more than you know. In fact, that leads me to the other thing I wanted to say."

"I can't wait to hear it."

"Drop the damn sarcasm and listen." His tone was low, almost urgent. "You need to know something, Sarah."

"Yeah?" she said warily. "And what's that?"

"I'm sorry."

Those two words came out strained, and his chest heaved, as if the mere act of uttering them had taken a physical toll on him.

Before she could reply, he hurried on. "I'm sorry for what happened between us. For the way I ended things. But you have to know that I didn't do it out of malice." He raked one hand through his tousled black hair. "I was young, Sarah. Young and scared and the situation was too familiar. It reminded me too much of what I went through with my..."

Mother, she nearly finished. She'd heard it all before, in the parting speech he'd recited before walking—no, *running*—out of her life. Oh, he'd run, all right. As if he was being chased by the damn bogeyman, as if her depression could infect him like some airborne disease.

Resentment prickled her skin. "I understand that the situation with your mom was messed up, Finn, but you weren't the only one with parent issues."

The memory of her own parents filtered into her

mind, bringing a rush of sorrow. She'd been orphaned at the age of four, after her parents died within months of each other, her mother in a car accident, her dad from a heart attack nobody saw coming. Her mother's older sister had taken Sarah in, but Aunt Carol hadn't been the most maternal woman. More like a hermit, locked away in her isolated house and painting dismal landscapes that usually featured black, ominous swamps or mountains shrouded by dark mist. Finn might have grown up with a mentally ill mother, but at least he'd had *someone*.

"And your past doesn't excuse the choices you made," she finished.

"It doesn't," he agreed, "but I'm trying to make amends for those choices now. I want to be here for you, Sarah. The way I wasn't back then. I'm going to get you out of this mess."

A myriad of emotions spun through her body. Anger. Pain. Hope. The last one grated the most, because she didn't want to hope. Didn't want to believe Finn's promise that he'd help her. He'd already proven that he couldn't be counted on. What if she put her life in his hands, the way she'd put her heart there, only to have him let her down again?

She couldn't. But she couldn't say no, either. Not when she had Lucy to think about. As much as it pained her to admit it, she did need him.

Yesterday, when Finn had mentioned the possibility of a trial, fear had streaked through her like a bolt of lightning. She couldn't go to trial. If she did, child welfare would snatch Lucy away faster than Sarah could say *wrongfully accused*. And there was no way she was giving up her baby. She'd waited two years for Lucy, and nobody was going to take her from Sarah.

And so she managed a silent nod of acceptance, unable to look at him.

He frowned again, sensing her reluctance, then released a humorless laugh. "You might not like it but I'm going to fix this, no matter what you say—or don't say—sweetheart."

A spark of heat tickled her spine. She had to force herself to snuff it out. So what if he'd called her sweetheart. So what if those two husky syllables reminded her of all those lazy mornings in bed, when he'd used that same word to cajole her into opening the gallery late so they could indulge in another round of hot, sweaty sex.

They were over. Done. And she refused to react to this man, no matter what he called her.

"Can you just call Anna so I can use the restroom?" she said abruptly.

His shoulders stiffened at her harsh tone, but before he could reply, a tentative female voice sounded from the end of the corridor.

"Sheriff?" Anna called. "I think you need to get up here."

"What's going on?" Finn called back, eyes narrowed.

"There's an FBI agent here. He says he's taking over the case."

Sarah noticed the visible shock on Finn's face. Without another look in her direction, he stalked off, his heavy black boots thudding against the cement floor.

Wariness climbed up her chest. An FBI agent had arrived to take over the case? On a Sunday?

That didn't sound good. At all.

When Finn marched into his office, he found a tall, fair-haired man in a crisp black business suit standing by the minuscule window overlooking the brick wall of the building next door. The man turned when the door opened, offering a tight smile as he said, "Sheriff Finnegan. Pleasure to meet you."

Finn advanced on the man, wincing when he noticed the grease-covered Chinese food containers littering his desktop and the white dress shirt slung over the back of his chair. He hadn't bothered to tidy up yet, and the slept-in office definitely didn't offer a good first impression.

But the agent made no mention of the mess, simply leaning forward for a handshake that Finn reluctantly returned. "I'm Special Agent Mark Parsons," the man added. "I've been asked to assist you on the Donovan investigation."

Finn smothered a curse. He could probably take a wild guess as to who had contacted the Bureau. Or maybe two guesses, since the M.O. fit both the mayor and district attorney of Serenade. Apparently, the bastards didn't trust him to stay impartial.

"Assist, huh? Because my deputy just said you told her you were here to take over the case."

Parsons's smile didn't even falter. Finn decided, right then and there, that he didn't like the guy. There was something predatory in those pale blue eyes, something that Finn frequently glimpsed in the D.A., that power-hungry glint characteristic of a man desperate to climb all the way to the top. He wondered if Parsons was new, some rookie looking to make a name for himself. Finn made a mental note to ask Jamie if she knew the man.

"She must have misunderstood me," Parsons said smoothly. "I simply relayed the instructions given to me by my supervisor—that this investigation required a new pair of eyes."

Since Anna had a better read on people than most psychics, Finn doubted his deputy had misunderstood. Parsons was here for one reason—to stick his nose into places it didn't belong and try to punch another notch in his glory belt.

Christ, and just when he thought things couldn't get any worse.

"Mayor Williams said we've got a suspect in custody."

Finn bristled at the *we*. "Yes, I arrested the owner of the town's art gallery yesterday. Sarah Connelly. Her hair was found at the scene, along with a partial fingerprint on the table near the body."

"Yes, I was informed of that, as well."

As Parsons sat on the edge of the sheriff's desk, making himself comfortable, Finn battled a burst of anger. He had no intention of working with this man. Parsons was too cocky, too smooth in his expensive suit. He had *slime bag* written all over him.

"I was also told there's still the matter of the murder weapon," Parsons went on in a brisk, professional voice. "So our first order of business is finding out exactly where the gun came from, and how it wound up in Connelly's hands."

"Look." Finn took a breath. "With all due respect, Agent Parsons, I'm not sure what you could possibly do that my staff and I haven't already done. The gun is untraceable, wiped of any prints. And if we're being forthcoming with each other, I have to tell you, I don't think Sarah Connelly killed Teresa Donovan."

A knowing glimmer entered Parson's eyes. "Does the fact that she's your ex-girlfriend have anything to do with that conviction?"

"No," Finn snapped. "But our past association does

come into play here. I *know* Sarah. She's not a killer. She runs a gallery, she's involved in community events, and she just adopted a baby. She's a good person."

"Good people have been known to snap and commit murder." Parsons stared at him with a condescending expression that made Finn want to deck the guy. "Sarah Connelly has a history of instability. She is certainly capable of killing Teresa Don—"

"So it's true!" a female voice shrieked.

Both men spun around to gape at the raven-haired woman who'd burst into the office without knocking.

Finn tamped down an irritated sigh as Valerie Matthews barreled toward him, her gunmetal-gray eyes blazing with what could only be described as perverse satisfaction. "I *knew* that crazy bitch was up to something! The way she befriended Agent Crawford so she could squeeze information out of her…"

Valerie trailed off deliberately, which only succeeded in pissing off Finn even further. Like her younger sister, Valerie was the nastiest, most unlikable woman Finn had ever met. She and Teresa had been two peas in a despicable pod, determined to make the lives of everyone around them miserable, as if that could make up for the crappy childhood they'd endured.

When Cole Donovan had been shot, Finn had actually begun to think that Valerie might have changed, that she was starting to let go of some of her craziness. Valerie had been knocked unconscious when Teresa's ex-lover had taken Jamie hostage, and when Finn visited her in the hospital, where she was being treated for a concussion, Valerie had been…pleasant. Sweet, even.

Looked like she was back to her old self.

"I expect you to send that woman to the gas chamber," Valerie spoke up, pure loathing in her voice.

"I'm not a judge," Finn answered with a sigh. "I can't sentence Sarah to death just because you demand it."

Those silver eyes fumed. "All I'm demanding is *justice*," she snapped. "I've been sitting around for a month, waiting for you and your incompetent department to find justice for my sister, and—"

"And now you have it," Agent Parsons cut in effortlessly.

Finn's hand tingled with the urge to punch the man in the jaw. "Isn't that a little premature to say, *Agent*? Sarah hasn't even been indicted yet."

But Valerie's entire face had lit up from Parsons's reassurance, and both of them ignored Finn as she stepped closer to the other man. "And who might you be?"

Finn stifled an incredulous groan. Flirting? She was flirting? During a discussion about her sister's *murder*?

"Special Agent Mark Parsons." Finn half expected the guy to puff out his chest like a damn peacock. "And you must be Valerie. Your name came up in the case file I read on the plane."

"So you're leading the investigation now?" She held her hand up to her heart. "Thank heavens. You don't know how long I've been waiting for someone to take charge."

It irked Finn like no tomorrow how Parsons didn't correct her, even though he'd "assured" Finn just minutes ago that he had no intention of taking over. It was clear the man hadn't meant a word of it, and even clearer that along with being a pretentious jackass, Parsons had a thing for trashy women.

"Don't you worry," Parsons drawled. "I'm here to make sure Connelly pays for her crimes."

Unable to stand there a second longer without throwing up, Finn stepped toward Valerie and placed a not-so-gentle hand on her arm. "You need to leave now," he told her. "Agent Parsons and I have a lot of work to do."

She spared him a pithy glance, then turned to Parsons and smiled sweetly. "Please keep me informed about the case."

"My pleasure."

Finn's jaw was tighter than a drum as he ushered Valerie out the door. Her high heels clicked against the tiled floor and as she disappeared into the corridor off the bull pen, Finn turned on his heel and frowned at the federal agent.

He'd had enough. The mayor was driving him insane, the D.A.'s smug certainty made him want to kick something, and now those two boneheads had deposited this unprofessional ass on his doorstep. His patience was beginning to wear thin and he feared he was nearing his breaking point. The very thought of Sarah stuck in that cell downstairs brought a hot wave of agony to his gut.

Powerless wasn't an emotion he did well. He'd always been tough, capable. Even when he didn't feel it, he put on the act, *daring* people to cross him. But right now, he felt out of control. Sarah was in trouble—and he couldn't seem to do a damn thing about it.

Well, it was time to change that.

His frown deepening, he advanced on the agent and snapped, "You shouldn't be discussing the case with anyone outside this office. Especially not with the victim's sister."

Parsons shrugged. "There's no harm in keeping the lady informed." He crossed his arms over the front of his tailored suit jacket. "Now, I'd like to go down to lockup and speak to Connelly."

A protective rush seized Finn's chest like a vise. No freaking way was he allowing this jerk to get within ten feet of Sarah. She was already emotional enough as it was, stuck in jail and separated from her daughter. Even a second with this pompous ass would undoubtedly fuel her anger. And when Sarah was angry, she ranted. And when she ranted, she often said things she shouldn't, things like, oh, *If you don't leave my daughter and me alone, you'll regret it.*

His lungs burned as he inhaled. Christ, she didn't know how bad this was. That one threat, whether she meant it or not, might very well seal her fate.

Unless Finn did something to help her.

But what?

Frustration coiled around his insides like barbed wire. Now that Parsons had entered the picture, saving Sarah would be drastically tougher. Not that he even had a plan. What he did have, though, was determination. Like he'd promised her, he was going to fix this, no matter what she said. He'd move heaven and earth for her. Sacrifice anyone or anything for her.

And maybe if he did that, maybe if he managed to get her out of this, he could finally, *finally* earn her forgiveness.

Chapter 4

Finn was uncomfortable as he entered Cole Donovan's kitchen a few hours later, and not just because the room was as big as the entire main floor of the farmhouse he lived in.

Although the two of them had joined forces to rescue Jamie from the clutches of Cole's crazed assistant, they weren't exactly the best of friends. Though Finn had to admit he was warming up to the guy. Donovan might be a multimillionaire, but he wasn't the arrogant ass Finn had previously believed him to be.

Parsons, on the other hand, *was* an arrogant ass, but Finn had made sure the federal agent was occupied for the afternoon. He'd told the man that learning more about the murder weapon was the most important task at hand. Fortunately, Parsons had agreed. He'd promptly forgotten about his intention to interrogate Sarah and was now meeting with the ballistics expert who'd handled the weapon.

With Parsons out of the way, Finn had left the station shortly after and headed to the lab, determined to make some headway of his own. But the talk with the lab tech had been not only unproductive, but a total spirit killer, as well.

"Want some coffee?" Cole asked, sounding awkward as they stepped into the kitchen.

Finn noticed that the other man was moving more slowly than usual—not surprising, seeing as he'd only been released from the hospital this morning and was still recovering from a bullet wound to the abdomen.

"Coffee would be great," Finn said, lowering himself onto one of the chairs at the table. He glanced at the doorway. "Jamie's upstairs with the baby?"

"Yeah. She'll be down soon. Lucy just woke up from her nap." Cole winced as he bumped his hip against the counter. He edged back, then reached for the coffeemaker.

Silence settled between them, which Finn used to try to come up with something to say. After Cole had been shot, Finn had promised himself that he'd try to be nicer to the guy, especially since Jamie was so obviously crazy about him.

She'd taken a leave of absence from the Bureau in order to be there for Cole's recovery, and you needed to be around the newly engaged couple for only ten seconds to see that they were madly in love.

"Lucy's a cute kid," Cole added as he poured hot coffee into two mugs. He turned to frown at Finn. "It's a damn shame what's happening to her mother. Did you really have to arrest her, Finnegan?"

Great, yet another name to add to the list of people who were pissed off at him.

Frowning right back, Finn took the cup Cole handed him and said, "I didn't have a choice. The evidence is pretty overwhelming."

To his surprise, Cole's dark eyes shone with sympathy. "But you don't think she did it."

"Hell, no." His throat clogged. "Sarah isn't capable of murder."

"Then prove it," came Jamie's blunt voice.

She appeared in the doorway, holding a sleepy-eyed Lucy in her arms. With her long auburn hair cascading down her back, her flawless makeup-free features and the yellow cotton dress dancing around her ankles, she made a seriously pretty picture. Finn wasn't the only one to notice, as Cole's rough face softened at the sight of her.

The couple exchanged a tender look that had Finn feeling like a damn Peeping Tom, then Jamie crossed the tiled floor and sat at the table. The baby let out a happy gurgle when she spotted Finn. His heart ached, then officially cracked when Lucy stretched out her chubby arms in his direction.

"She wants you to hold her," Jamie said with a grin, already moving the baby onto his lap.

He instinctively pulled Lucy against his chest, strands of emotion unraveling inside him as she lifted her head and stared at him with big brown eyes.

"I swear, she has the sunniest disposition," Jamie remarked, watching as the baby reached up to touch Finn's chin. "I'm already in love with her and I've only had her for a few hours."

Finn found himself going motionless as Sarah's daughter explored his face. She scrunched her tiny nose when her fingers met the stubble coating his jaw. With the curiosity that only a child could possess, she touched the sharp whiskers on his face, then gurgled in delight, as if discovering a new texture she couldn't believe existed.

Warmth spread through him. A lump rose in the back of his throat. Lord, this angelic little girl could have been his. If he hadn't abandoned Sarah, this could have been their future.

Shame exploded in his gut, making it difficult to breathe. Regrets were a side effect of life, he knew that. Everyone had something they regretted, some mistake they wished they hadn't made, but his regret…his mistake…it consumed his entire life. It moved like poison through his bloodstream, pricked his skin like tiny needles.

How could he have thrown away the woman he loved?

"How's Sarah doing?" Jamie asked, oblivious to his inner turmoil.

"Good, considering," he said. "She's eager to go home, but the bail hearing won't be until tomorrow morning."

Cole came to the table, handing Jamie a cup of coffee before joining them. "I still don't get it," the man said, shaking his head. "How did Sarah's DNA turn up at the crime scene?" He paused. "Could it have been a mistake? A lab error?"

"There was no error. I just came from the lab." His stomach clenched. "I spoke to Tom Hannigan, had him talk me through the results. The fingerprint on the coffee table is a perfect match to Sarah. So is the DNA extracted from the hair sample. She was in the house, according to the evidence."

"Evidence which could have been planted," Jamie pointed out. "If Sarah says she never stepped foot in Teresa's house, I believe her."

"Me, too," Finn admitted.

"So that means that someone took it upon themselves to put her hair there."

"And the print?"

Jamie went silent. They both knew how tricky it would be to plant someone's fingerprint. By no means impossible, but it would take a lot of careful planning to make something like that happen.

Frustration simmered in his stomach. "I just can't figure out who would want to frame her, or why. I get why someone would try and frame Cole—"

"Thanks," Cole cut in with a grimace.

"You're the ex-husband," Finn said without apologizing. "The most obvious suspect. If the killer wanted to take the heat off himself and put it on someone else, you're the best bet. Sarah had no connection to Teresa. There's no reason for someone to frame her."

"No reason we know of," Jamie said. She made an annoyed sound. "What are we missing here? We've got a list a mile long of people who didn't like Teresa. Why can't we connect anyone to her murder?"

Finn had no reply. God knows he and his deputies had been working their butts off interviewing people in town, trying to find puzzle pieces that might help them construct the bigger picture, but this case refused to move forward. All they had was an untraceable murder weapon and evidence placing Sarah at the scene.

"I still think we need to look at Teresa's lovers," Jamie added. "Look what she did to Ian Macintosh—she completely messed up his head and turned him into an enraged stalker. It's not a stretch to think she manipulated someone else."

"Well, the only other man we know she was involved with was Parker Smith," Finn answered. "And he has an airtight alibi for the night Teresa died." He glanced at Cole. "Did you manage to come up with another name? Anyone else she may have been involved with?"

Cole slowly shook his head. "No. I have my private investigator on it, but he hasn't turned anything up, either. I'll give him a call and see if he's managed to make headway, but I don't think—"

Finn's foghorn ring tone interrupted. With great reluctance, he handed Lucy back to Jamie and pulled his cell phone from his pocket. The station's number flashed on the screen.

"Finnegan," he said brusquely.

"Sheriff, it's me," came Anna's voice. "You told me to let you know what's going on with Sarah, and—"

"Is she all right?" he interrupted.

"She's fine. But she does have a visitor. Dr. Bennett. I figured you'd want to know."

Dr. Bennett?

"Oh. Okay, thanks for letting me know, Anna." He hung up, wrinkling his forehead.

"Is something wrong?" Jamie asked instantly.

"No." He paused, still confused. "Apparently Sarah has a visitor, though. It's Travis Bennett."

"The doctor who runs the clinic?" When Finn nodded, Jamie tilted her head, pensive. "He's a nice man. He treated me after the car accident. I didn't know they were friends, though."

"Yeah, me, neither."

He was helpless to stop the jolt of jealousy that pounded into his gut. Granted, he had no right feeling jealous. Sarah could be friends with whomever she pleased. He'd given up the right to have a say in her life when he'd walked out that door. But he had been keeping tabs on her all these years, and this was the first he'd heard of a connection between her and Bennett.

Were they involved?

Another hot blade of jealousy sliced into him. Travis Bennett was older, late forties at least, but he was still an attractive man, in a bland kind of way. He'd moved to Serenade three years ago from Raleigh, after losing his wife and two sons in a tragic fire. Finn had researched the guy when he had showed up in town—he always made sure to know everything about the people he served—and he'd learned that the doctor had left a booming practice to open his small clinic here. He'd been grief-stricken when he'd first arrived, barely speaking a word to anyone, but he'd eventually opened up, and the folks in town loved him.

He wondered what *Sarah* thought of the good doctor, then clamped down the inappropriate rush of anger.

Abruptly, he scraped his chair back and got to his feet. "I should get going," he muttered. "Thanks for the coffee."

Jamie and Cole both wore knowing expressions. Apparently the reason for his sudden departure was clear to all.

Ignoring the looks, he glanced at Lucy, the hardness in his body thawing as he reached to stroke the downy black hair atop her small head. "Be good for Jamie, baby girl," he murmured.

She rewarded him with a big, toothless smile.

"I'll keep you guys posted," he said to the couple at the table. "Take good care of her, Jamie. Sarah's counting on you."

Her violet eyes softened, but he strode to the door before she could respond. He didn't need her reassurance—he knew Jamie would love and care for Lucy as if she were her own daughter.

And in the meantime, he would take care of Lucy's mother.

"Are you sure there isn't anything I can do?" Travis Bennett asked in a voice laced with concern. "I still have contacts in Raleigh, some attorney friends. I can give one of them a call—"

"It's fine," Sarah cut in, forcing a smile. "I already hired a lawyer, and I'm sure he'll manage to get me out on bail tomorrow morning."

Travis didn't look appeased. His deep-set brown eyes shone with compassion, and she realized that's what probably made him such an excellent doctor. When he'd first moved to town, she'd thought him cold and unfeeling, until the day she'd caught a nasty chest infection and had been forced to visit his clinic. One minute with Dr. Travis Bennett and she'd realized he truly was a good man. Hadn't bothered looking for a new doctor, either. He'd been the first person she'd called when Lucy had come down with an ear infection last month, and like the caring person he was, Travis had made a house call and personally delivered Lucy's antibiotics.

And now he was here, trying to make everything better.

But there was nothing he or anyone else could do. Scratch that—the only person who could help her now was Judge Rollins, if he managed to step away from the damn golf course.

"I don't understand why the sheriff is keeping you locked up in the first place," Travis said.

"He's just doing his job," she said darkly.

"Well, he's got the wrong person behind bars. I want you to know I don't think you killed that woman, Sarah. And if you change your mind and need my help, all you have to do is call."

Finn's voice came from behind. "Sorry for interrupting." He strode down the corridor and stood in front of the cell, eyeing Dr. Bennett with displeasure. "What brings you here, Doc?"

Travis frowned. "I saw you leaving the lab earlier and asked Tom Hannigan what was going on. He informed me that Sarah is in police custody."

"Tom shouldn't have spoken to you about that," Finn said coldly.

"We work in the same building, Sheriff. We speak frequently." The doctor turned to Sarah. "I should probably go. Let me know if you need anything."

"I'll walk you out," Finn said, sounding anything but cordial.

Sighing, Sarah watched as the two men disappeared from sight. She hadn't missed the glitter of anger in Finn's blue eyes. It was an expression she was familiar with, yet one she hadn't seen in years. Finn had always been a possessive man, not in a creepy, violent way, but just a male making his claim. He'd donned that *back off* look whenever men in town got a little too friendly with her. Back then, she'd found it flattering.

Right now, it simply annoyed her.

"So," Finn said when he returned a few moments later. "Since when are you and Bennett so tight?"

Her nostrils flared. What right did he have getting angry over her friendship with Travis? Or even asking questions about it? He'd given up his claim on her a long time ago.

"That's not any of your business," she answered coolly.

"He's almost twice your age," Finn grumbled.

A shocked laugh escaped her lips. "So what? Travis is a friend. Who cares how old he is?"

Those dark eyebrows rose slightly. "Just a friend?"

"Yes, though I really don't need to explain myself to you." She spun on her heel and made her way to the cot, flopping down and avoiding Finn's eyes. She figured he'd just walk away, but he surprised her by unlocking the cell door and marching inside.

"Get up," he muttered. "I've got dinner in my office."

Surprise moved through her. "You're letting me go upstairs?"

Pure misery flashed in his eyes. "I'm not your warden, Sarah. No matter what you think, it kills me seeing you in here, okay?"

Her throat went tight. Sincerity rang in his voice, and there was no mistaking the pain flickering across his face. No, she supposed he didn't like this any more than she did. The only difference was—*she* was the one in this position. Not him.

Story of their lives, wasn't it? She fell apart, and he stood there, strong and stoic in the background.

She straightened her shoulders, banishing that pang of self-pity from her head. Screw that. She *was* strong. She might have fallen apart all those years ago, but this time she refused to cave under the pressure. She'd been arrested for a crime she didn't commit, and she'd be damned if she didn't keep fighting this injustice until her last breath.

Without a word, she stood and followed Finn out of the cell.

"I saw your daughter," he said as they climbed the narrow staircase.

Sarah almost tripped over her own feet at the quiet confession. Unable to stop herself, she looked directly into his vivid blue eyes. "You did? Is she all right?"

"She's fine," he said gruffly. "Jamie said Lucy is the sweetest baby in the world."

Tears stung her eyes. "I know."

She tried to rein in her emotions as they headed to Finn's office. The bull pen was empty, so fortunately she didn't have to face the curious eyes of Anna or Finn's second deputy, Max. Blinking a few times, she took a deep breath and sat down in one of the chairs in front of Finn's cluttered desk.

He'd gotten takeout from the diner—she recognized the brown paper bags with Martha's red logo printed on them. Neither of them said a word as they tackled their food, though Sarah felt Finn's eyes on her as she ate. Was he thinking about the last time they'd shared a meal together?

She was trying not to, but the excruciating memory found its way into her brain no matter how hard she tried to stop it.

You don't want to be here, do you?

She heard her own voice in her head, the lifeless words she'd uttered, the anger that followed.

Leave then. Take the coward's way out and leave!

She'd proceeded to throw his plate against the wall, staining the white wall with spaghetti sauce, sending clumps of noodles onto the hardwood floor. And then she'd sunk onto the floor herself, as hot tears poured down her cheeks, as she cried for everything they'd lost and everything he refused to give her.

"I shouldn't have left that night."

His rough voice sliced through her thoughts, and she realized as she met his tortured expression that he had indeed been thinking the same thing.

"But you did," she said flatly, pushing away her half-eaten dinner.

Finn reached for the bottle of water on the desk, unscrewed the cap and took a long swallow. After he set down the bottle, he continued to speak, his blue eyes avoiding her face.

"My mom used to do that, during her episodes. She'd curl up into a ball on the floor and sob, and I would stand there, unable to do a damn thing about it. I tried to comfort her once, but she slapped me so hard I never did it again." His voice cracked. "I didn't know what to do, when I saw you like that."

Her lungs burned so badly she could barely get out any words. "So you left."

"I left," he echoed. "And I've regretted it every day, every damn second, of these last four years."

Sarah couldn't look at him. She couldn't go down this path. It had taken two years of therapy to convince her that her reaction to everything that happened had been natural. That sometimes even the strongest of people collapsed under the strain. But it was still hard to reflect on that time in her life and not feel shame. Embarrassment.

Why hadn't she been stronger?

Why hadn't *he* been stronger?

"Sarah, look at me."

She swallowed, blinking through a shimmer of tears. *No, don't look at him.* She couldn't. This man had crushed her. He'd left her battered and broken and hadn't even looked back.

His hand was on her face.

Her head jerked in shock. She hadn't even heard him get up, yet here he was, on his knees in front of her chair, his warm, calloused hands cupping her chin. Forcing eye contact.

Breathing hard, she met his gaze and was floored by what she saw there. Regret. Anguish. Passion. Always with the passion. From the moment they'd collided into each other at the lake, the attraction between them had been impossible to control.

Even now, when she ought to despise him, when she ought to be concentrating on her own self-preservation, her body reacted to Finn. Her palms went damp, her breasts became heavy, and the tender spot between her legs began to throb.

"Sarah…"

His timber-rough voice sent a shiver along her spine. She felt the heat of his body, searing right through the thin material of her turtleneck.

His strong throat worked as he swallowed. "I miss you."

Shock filled her chest. The longing surrounding those three words stole the breath right out of her lungs. She struggled to inhale, but then Finn's head moved closer, closer, until his warm breath fanned over her mouth.

Until she knew without a doubt that he was going to kiss her.

Chapter 5

He was lost in Sarah. Drowning in the intoxicating lilac scent of her, the sight of her tousled dark hair, the way her lush lips parted in surprise. Finn's heart drummed a frenzied rhythm against his ribs. Every muscle in his body went taut, rippling with anticipation, with need so strong his vision grew cloudy. But through the haze, he still saw her. Sarah. His Sarah, with her high, regal cheekbones and satin-soft skin and that sweet, sensual mouth.

He leaned closer.

He wanted to kiss her. Just once. Just to see if that uncontrollable fire between them still burned strong.

His lips hovered over hers. He could almost taste her. Almost feel the softness of her mouth—

Her chair scraped back with a loud grating sound.

"No, Finn. *No*." Her voice contained a hint of desperation, a twinge of confusion.

Disappointment rushed through him like a flash flood. His hands shook as he staggered to his feet, the promise of reconnecting with Sarah blown away by the ragged breath that exited his mouth.

"I'm sorry," he rasped. "I didn't mean to do that."

Yes, you did.

Fine. He'd wanted to kiss her. For four very long years.

But she'd wanted it, too. He'd seen the desire swimming in her brown eyes. Heard her intake of breath. Seen her pulse throbbing in her graceful neck. He'd witnessed those same telltale signs years ago, the day they'd met at the lake, as he'd walked her to where she'd parked her car. He didn't normally make a move on women he'd just met, but something about Sarah had made him delirious with desire, desperate to feel her mouth pressed to his.

He'd kissed her, right there in the little gravel parking lot near the lakeshore, and when they'd pulled apart, she'd given a little laugh and asked him if he was always that forward. The attraction to Sarah had been daunting. She was gentle, smart, her eyes always full of laughter; he was serious, easily angered, a loner. He hadn't expected to fall in love with someone like Sarah. Hell, back then he'd gravitated toward bold, flashy women like Teresa Donovan.

But from the moment he'd heard Sarah's soft, throaty voice, from the moment he'd brushed his lips over her warm, sexy mouth, he'd been a goner.

And still was.

"Whether you meant it or not, it can't happen again," she said in a shaky voice. "I won't let it happen."

His legs felt weak, limp, so he leaned against the edge of the desk, casting a sad look in her direction.

She'd pretty much flattened herself against the wall, as if expecting him to ambush her at any second. But she didn't look scared, just wary, and that was far more disheartening.

"Would it be so bad?" he had to ask. "Starting over?"

Her eyebrows knitted in disbelief. "Starting over?" she echoed. "We can't start over, Finn."

His heart dropped to the pit of his stomach like a sinking rock. "Because I left."

"Because I don't trust you. Because I can't forget."

Her quiet admission grabbed hold of his heart and twisted it in his chest. Hard. He wasn't sure he'd ever experienced such overwhelming pain.

"And forgiveness? Can you forgive?" he found himself murmuring, practically holding his breath for her answer.

She sighed, her rigid shoulders sagging into a posture that resembled defeat. "I forgave you a long time ago, Finn."

His gaze flew to hers. "You did?"

She nodded. "But that doesn't change anything."

"It's something," he said hoarsely.

"It's nothing," she corrected, her voice equally hoarse.

Their gazes locked. She meant it, he realized, as frustration filled his gut and sorrow knotted around his insides. And she was right. Her forgiveness meant nothing, not if the trust she'd once had in him was gone.

"Okay." He cleared his throat. "Okay, then at least I know what to do now."

She glanced at him, wary again. "And what's that?"

"Make you trust me again."

The pressure weighing down on his chest lifted a little. All wasn't lost. Her lack of faith in him hurt, but it only gave him something to strive toward. She hadn't said she hated him, hadn't disregarded the chemistry they evidently still shared. If this was about trust, then he could work with that. He could fix it.

A tired laugh slipped from her lips. "You never give up, do you, Finn?"

"I did once," he said, holding her gaze. "I gave up on us. But I promise you, sweetheart, I won't do it again. I'm older. Wiser. And if it's the last thing I do in my miserable life, I'm going to win your trust back."

His declaration got to her. He could see it in her eyes. Some of the tension had even left her body. Not the wariness, but he would change that.

"I can't talk about this right now," she finally said. "I have bigger problems to deal with."

"I know, and I promise that—"

"Well, isn't this cozy."

They both looked at the door, just as Agent Mark Parsons strode into the office as if he owned the place. Finn's jaw instantly tensed, a spurt of anger erupting in his belly as Parsons studied the scene with condescending eyes. Finn knew what it looked like—remnants of their dinner on his desk, Sarah out of her cell. He didn't feel an ounce of remorse, though. Maybe he was giving her preferential treatment, but Parsons could go to hell.

With a smile that didn't quite reach his eyes, Parsons turned to Sarah. "You must be Ms. Connelly."

She stole a glance at Finn, then focused on the federal agent. "Yes…"

"I'm Special Agent Mark Parsons." He made a move to extend his hand, then stopped when he saw the look in Sarah's eyes.

Finn bit back a laugh. He knew that look. It said *touch me and I'll rip your eyes out*. He remembered being on the receiving end of it plenty of times, usually when he pissed Sarah off by forgetting to load the dishwasher or leaving his wet towels on the bathroom floor.

Parsons continued as if Sarah's rebuff hadn't affected him, but the annoyed flicker in his pale blue eyes told another story. "I must admit, I was looking forward to meeting you this morning, but the sheriff wasn't so open to the idea. I'm assuming that's why he sent me on what he believed would be a wild goose chase."

Finn didn't bother trying to look repentant. Had he wanted to keep Parsons away from Sarah? Hell yes. Had he sent him on a task that he knew would probably amount to noth—wait a second. He suddenly realized what the agent had said. *What he believed would be a wild goose chase.*

Parsons offered a pleasant smile. "That's right, Sheriff. I happened to uncover something on my assignment today."

Finn stifled a sigh. "Maybe I should take Ms. Connelly back to her cell so you and I can—"

"No need for that," Parsons interrupted. "I'd like to question her about this anyway, so we might as well do it now. Have a seat, Ms. Connelly."

With a suspicious cloud in her eyes, Sarah sat down in the visitor's chair, while Parsons took her place by the wall, his arms crossed over his lanky chest. Finn stayed by the desk, too wound up to move. He didn't like the expression on the agent's face. Parsons resembled a predator about to go in for a kill.

"As the sheriff probably told you," Parsons began, his tone implying that Finn was whispering police pillow talk in Sarah's ear, "I've been tracking the origins of the weapon that killed Mrs. Donovan. A .45 Smith & Wesson."

If Parsons had been expecting a reaction from Sarah, he didn't get it. Rather, she shot him a cool look and said, "And?"

"I still haven't been able to trace it, but I did come across some very interesting information...."

There was a long pause, which only irritated the hell out of Finn. "What did you find?" he snapped.

"Your deputies checked if any weapons matching that make and description had been reported stolen in Serenade."

"And nothing came up in the system," Finn retorted.

"No," Parsons agreed. "But I used the Bureau's database to search other precincts in the area to see if any missing weapon reports popped up." Parsons gave a smug smile. "A man in Grayden, your neighboring town, reported a .45 Smith & Wesson missing about a month ago. Four days before Mrs. Donovan was murdered, in fact."

Finn refused to let the other man see just how much the new information rattled him. "So?" he said, putting on a bored face. "What's the connection, other than the make of the gun?"

"Turns out this man, a Mr. Walter Brown, used to work at the paper mill that Cole Donovan tore down when he moved here." The federal agent smirked. "Apparently, Mr. Brown keeps in touch with some of his old friends here in town. The night his gun was stolen, he was hosting a party to celebrate a promotion at his new position in Grayden's textile factory."

Finn got a sick feeling in his stomach.

"And he claims that several Serenade citizens attended the festivities," Parsons finished, looking so damn pleased with himself that Finn wanted to clock him. The agent glanced at Sarah. "Did you happen to be in attendance, Ms. Connelly?"

Her shoulders stiffened. "No, I was not in attendance. I don't even know Walter Brown."

"Interesting." Parsons cocked his head. "Because I pulled your credit card records for the time period in question, and what do you know, you purchased gas at a station in Grayden—the same day as Brown's party."

Finn's heart dropped. From the defensive flicker in Sarah's eyes, he knew Parsons was telling the truth. She'd been in Grayden that day.

"I was visiting an artist," Sarah finally admitted. Hostility hardened her features as she stared Parsons down. "His name is Frank Bullocks, you can call him up and he'll confirm that we met that day."

"Oh, I will definitely be giving him a call, Ms. Connelly. Tell me, how long did this visit last?"

She shrugged. "An hour, maybe two. He showed me some of his new pieces, and I took a few back to the gallery. He's one of the artists I have on consignment. I can't say for sure what I did when I got home, but I know I never went back to Grayden that night—and I didn't attend some stranger's party."

"If you say so."

Finn dragged a hand through his hair, then moved from his perch on the desk. "I'm going to take Sarah back to her cell now."

"I'm not done with her, Sher—"

He silenced Parsons by raising his hand. "She answered your questions and explained why she was in Grayden that day. You can follow up with Brown and get a guest list from him. If Sarah's name happens to be on it, you'll get another chance to speak to her. But right now, I'm taking Ms. Connelly to her cell."

He didn't wait for another objection, simply took Sarah's arm and led her out of his office. In the bull pen, she opened her mouth to speak, but he used that same silencing hand. She didn't try again until they were descending the narrow staircase leading down to lockup.

"This is bad, isn't it?" she said in a hushed voice. "They're going to say I stole the gun from that man's house and used it to kill Teresa! God, Finn, you can't let that happen! I didn't steal anything!"

He heard her panic, saw the fear trembling in her shoulders, and before she could protest, he yanked her into his arms.

She went rigid for one long moment, then sank into the embrace, pressing her face against the front of his blue buttondown. Pure joy spread inside him, warming every inch of his body. She was in his arms again, and that feeling of *rightness* nearly knocked him over like a gust of wind.

Stroking her lower back with his hands, he held her, breathing in the sweet scent of her hair. "This is bad," he murmured against the top of her head. "I can't deny that, but I told you I was going to fix this. I promised you, Sarah."

She burrowed her face in the crook of his neck. Moisture coated his skin. She was crying. Lord, it tore him up, feeling her tears soak his flesh. The last time she'd cried, he'd walked out the door.

This time, he just held her tighter.

"Did you take your pain meds?"

Cole Donovan stifled a groan as his fiancée appeared in the doorway just as he'd been shoving the prescription bottle into the top drawer of their night-stand. Jamie's lavender eyes instantly zeroed in on his hand, and a frown marred her mouth. *Damn it, caught red-handed.*

"Don't you dare hide the pills again," she said, swooping into the bedroom with Sarah's daughter in her arms. "I don't get you, you know that? You just had surgery to remove a bullet from your stomach. You're in pain. Quit pretending otherwise."

Despite himself, he smiled. He couldn't remember the last time someone had fussed over him like this. His mother had always been too drunk to notice he was even around, his father was never home, and Teresa had been the furthest thing from a doting wife. He had to admit, it was kind of nice that Jamie was so concerned about him.

"Take the bottle out and swallow the damn pills," she ordered, shifting the baby onto her other hip.

Knowing when he was beaten, Cole obeyed her with-out argument. As he picked up the glass of water she'd brought in earlier and took the pills, he couldn't help but admire the way she skillfully held the baby. A natural mother. A rush of tenderness filled his body. He almost forgot about the pain throbbing in his wounded abdo-men as he realized that one of these days he and Jamie would have a baby of their own. She wanted children. Lots of them.

And he couldn't wait to give them to her.

"There, I did it," he said after he'd taken his meds. "But you can't complain when I'm too stoned to hold a conversation with you."

"I can talk to Lucy," Jamie said with a shrug. She

tickled the baby's tummy, eliciting a delighted gurgle. "Right, sweet pea? We'll do all the talking tonight."

Cole slid down in the bed and rested his head against the pillow. Damn, those meds worked fast. His head was already beginning to feel light.

"I'm just going to warm a bottle for her," Jamie said. "I'll come up and feed her here. And remember, you're bed-bound. I made an exception when Finn was here earlier, but now you're back to following the doctor's orders."

"Yes, ma'am."

As Jamie disappeared through the doorway, Cole smiled again, wondering how he'd gotten so damn lucky. When Jamie had waltzed into town two weeks ago, he'd never dreamed that he'd fall in love with the federal agent who was supposed to profile him. Never dreamed he'd fall in love, period. After his marriage to Teresa, the thought of being in another relationship had left him in a cold sweat. But Jamie had changed all that.

He could hear her moving around downstairs, the muffled sound of her voice, broken in by Lucy's happy squeals. Lord, he felt terrible for Sarah Connelly. Sarah had always been so nice to him, even after he'd closed down the paper mill and built a hotel in its place, enraging everyone in town. But not Sarah. She'd treated him with nothing but kindness, and she didn't deserve what was happening to her.

A thud came from below.

Cole sat up, fighting a rush of dizziness. The lethargic numbness the meds provided him with made it hard to think clearly, but he still managed a quick shout. "You okay down there, sweetheart?"

He heard another crash, followed by a loud cry that hadn't come from the baby. Jamie!

Cole launched himself out of bed. The world spun for a moment, his vision assaulted by stars. He steadied himself, forced his legs to carry him to the door, as panic shuddered through him and fear coursed in his blood. He could hear Lucy wailing now, but it sounded tinny and faraway in his drugged state. He experienced another burst of vertigo at the top of the staircase. Breathed through it. Stumbled down the stairs.

"Jamie!" he shouted. "Lucy!"

He raced into the kitchen, ignoring the searing pain shooting up his abdomen. "Jamie. Ja—" His voice died in his throat as he caught sight of her.

"Oh, Jesus…" He was down on the floor, kneeling beside her motionless figure. His pulse shrieked in his ears. "Jamie, baby, wake up!"

She was on her side, and he quickly rolled her over, running his hands along her body, across her face. When he touched her hair, he felt dampness beneath his palm. He lifted his hand and saw blood. Someone had hit her in the crown of the head.

"Jamie," he pleaded. "Open your eyes, sweetheart."

She moaned. It was the sweetest sound he'd ever heard in his entire life. And then her lids fluttered open, and her violet eyes, those beautiful eyes, stared up at him in confusion.

"C-Cole?"

"I'm here, sweetheart. I'm here. Tell me what happened."

Wincing, she struggled to sit up. "I…the bottle…" She glanced in the direction of the sink. He followed her gaze, immediately spotting the broken bottle. A puddle of milk had formed on the tiled floor.

A loud bang made them jump, and they both turned to the patio door, which was wide open and being blown against the exterior wall by the wind.

An anguished cry left Jamie's mouth. "Lucy!" She sat up, shoving hair out of her eyes. "Cole, he took the baby!"

Chapter 6

The Donovan house was deathly silent when Finn hurried inside. Driving over in his Jeep with the siren blaring, he'd conjured up dozens of terrifying scenes he might find, everything from bloodstained walls to Jamie dead on the floor. What he found, however, was much worse. Four shell-shocked faces greeted him when he entered the living room, Jamie the most distraught of all.

She was on the overstuffed leather sofa closest to the bay window that overlooked the front yard, tears staining her face as she leaned against Cole for support. Finn noticed Cole looked unusually pale, but that was probably because his fiancée had just been knocked unconscious while he lay upstairs doped up on pain meds.

At least that's what Max had relayed to Finn over the phone. Finn hadn't said a word to Sarah before he'd rushed out of the station. He didn't want to worry her, especially when the only detail he'd been given was *Lucy's gone!*

His two deputies, Anna and Max, were already on the scene, and he could hear his forensics guy, Chris, puttering around in the kitchen. Five adults in the house, six including him—but no baby.

"He took her!" Jamie blurted out when she spotted Finn in the doorway. "He came up from behind… I didn't even hear him… I'm so sorry, Finn, I'm so sorry."

He bounded across the parquet floor and sat on the other side of her, stroking her arm in a soothing motion. "Jamie, calm down. Tell me what happened."

"I was preparing a bottle for Lucy." She wheezed out an unsteady breath. "I set her down in her bouncy seat and then went to get the bottle. I was checking to see that the formula wasn't too hot when I heard the back door open. I turned around, but he moved too fast. All I saw was a black ski mask. I had no time to react. He was holding something, a crowbar maybe, and he knocked me out."

Finn frowned. "He just walked through the back door? The alarm didn't go off?"

Jamie's face collapsed like a house of cards. "I forgot to set it. I was so busy today, trying to put Lucy down for her nap, and then making sure Cole took his pills. I…forgot."

A current of guilt thrashed in her lavender eyes. It was evident to everyone in the room that she blamed herself for what had happened. Both Anna and Max were staring down at their feet, waves of sympathy radiating from them. Cole looked devastated, as if he couldn't believe he'd failed to protect the two females in his house.

"Don't beat yourself up over it," Finn said quietly. "People forget to do things sometimes. Happens to the best of us."

"Not to me," Jamie said bleakly. "I'm a federal agent, Finn. I don't forget to set security systems! God, this is all my fault. Sarah... How am I going tell Sarah?"

Oh, Christ. Sarah. The sound of her name made his gut go rigid. He'd spent all evening with her in the cell, comforting her after Parsons had dropped the new information about the murder weapon in their laps. She'd been so upset, terrified that the case against her was only getting stronger. How on earth would she react when she discovered someone had kidnapped her daughter?

Finn pushed away the unsettling thought and focused on his friend, who looked as though she was struggling not to cry.

"This isn't your fault, Jamie. Whoever took Lucy knew what he was doing. He had a purpose when he came in—he wanted the baby." Finn searched her face. "Are you sure it was a man?"

She wrinkled her forehead in despair. "I don't know. Like I said, I didn't get a good look. He just sprang up on me like some kind of ninja. I guess I just assumed it was a man."

"How tall was the assailant?"

"Around my height, give or take an inch."

Finn thought it over. Jamie was five-nine, so if the intruder was male, he stood slightly below average height. And if it was a female, then she was taller than most women.

"I guess it could have been a woman," Jamie relented, looking miserable. "But I really couldn't tell. It all happened too damn fast."

"Did he or she say anything?" Anna asked.

"Nothing," Jamie said. "And if he did, I couldn't hear it. All I heard was Lucy crying."

Finn sighed. "Okay. Well, we need to get an Amber Alert out, contact the media." He glanced at Max, who was standing by the tall bookshelf across the high-ceilinged room. "I need you to canvas the neighborhood, call in our volunteer unit and comb every inch of this damn town."

"Yes, sir," Max said, already heading for the door.

He turned to Anna. "Get back to the station, start working the phones. We need to get the alert out, make sure everyone and their mother knows what Lucy looks like and that she's been abducted."

Anna responded with a nod, quickly getting up and hurrying out of the room. Thank God for his deputies, at least. At twenty-four, Anna was unbelievably efficient, always able to keep a cool head no matter the chaos around her. Max was a year younger and more of a renegade, often acting without thinking things through, but always giving one-hundred-and-ten percent in every situation. At the moment, Finn appreciated the knowledge that he had two capable people working the case.

Sarah was going to be destroyed. Hell, he felt pretty destroyed himself. He'd held Lucy in his arms only hours ago, and now she was gone.

Jamie's ravaged voice broke through his thoughts. "I messed up."

He saw the moisture gathering in her eyes and squeezed her arm. "It's okay. We'll find her, Jamie."

She simply stared down into her lap, unconvinced. Finn regarded Cole over Jamie's head, and the two men exchanged a somber look. Jamie was the toughest woman Finn knew, but she also had the biggest heart. She'd never forgive herself for letting Lucy get taken, no matter what anyone else said.

Cole gave an imperceptible nod, as if to reassure Finn that he would take care of Jamie.

Nodding back, Finn rose from the sofa. "I should call Agent Parsons. Maybe he can get things moving faster."

Jamie's head snapped up. "Wait a minute—Mark Parsons? He's in town?"

The disdain in her voice didn't go unmissed. "You know him?" Finn said warily.

A frown puckered her lips. "Yeah, I know him. Why is he here?"

"Mayor Williams called in a favor. Apparently, he thinks I need help with the case."

Jamie let out a soft curse, suddenly looking more like herself. Her cheeks took on some color, as displeasure glittered in her eyes. "I feel sorry for you, then. That guy is a total jackass."

"That's what I was afraid you'd say," he admitted. "I take it you don't like him."

"He lives in a tunnel," Jamie grumbled.

Finn shot her a blank look.

"Tunnel vision," she clarified. "He's got a reputation for it in the office. He gets his teeth into a suspect and doesn't bother examining any other avenues. It's gotten him in trouble a few times."

"So you're saying once he thinks he's got his man, he quits investigating?"

"Pretty much, yeah."

Wonderful. Sarah didn't stand a chance then.

Sarah.

For a moment there, he'd actually forgotten about

her. About the fact that someone had just *abducted* her daughter.

How the hell was he going to break the news to Sarah?

When Finn walked into her cell that night, Sarah sensed something terrible had happened. After the bomb Agent Parsons had dropped about the murder weapon earlier, Finn had spent an hour in her cell, attempting to comfort her and calm her down. As hard as she'd tried not to lean on him, she hadn't been able to control herself. She hadn't been in his arms for so long, she'd almost forgotten how strong he was. How sheltered she felt when he held her. He was so big, so masculine. She'd always felt safe in his embrace, soothed by his presence.

But it didn't soothe her now. His blue eyes were wrought with tension, his hair mussed up, as if he'd ran his fingers through it a hundred times. Unease filled her belly, congealing into a hard knot as Finn came up to her cot and sat down beside her. Not even the feel of his hard thigh pressed against her much softer one could ease her anxiety.

"What's wrong?" she asked instantly, turning her head to meet his shuttered eyes.

"Sarah..." His husky voice trailed off, which only heightened her alarm.

"Finn, what's going on?"

"I...I don't even know how to say it."

Her pulse quickened, prompting her to stumble to her feet. She stared at him, studied the deep groove in his forehead. She knew that groove. It only appeared when he was truly upset about something. Last time she'd seen it, he'd been telling her he was leaving. This time, she got the feeling the news was much, much worse.

"Tell me," she ordered, pressing her suddenly damp palms to her sides.

"Lucy's gone."

The floor beneath her feet seemed to crumble away as if the ground had split open. As her knees gave out, she staggered back to the cot before she fell over. Her ears started to ring, so loudly that she had to wonder if maybe she'd misheard him.

Hope tickled her chest. Of course she'd misheard him. She *must* have. Because no way could he have just told her that—

"She was abducted from Cole and Jamie's house an hour ago."

The world began to spin. "No," she choked out. "No, you're lying."

She felt his warm hand on her knee. "I'm sorry, sweetheart. I wish I didn't have to tell you this. I wish I could assure you that Lucy is safe and sound, in Jamie's arms. I wish…"

An incredible force of anger slammed into her body, prompting her to fling his hand off her. This couldn't be happening. It *couldn't* be. How could Lucy be gone? Why would someone have taken her? It didn't make sense.

Terror burned a path up her throat, lodging into a painful lump. She couldn't even draw in a breath. Couldn't move.

"How…" She spoke through the pressure in her chest. "How did this happen? How could you *let* this happen?"

Finn flinched as if she'd struck him, but she didn't

feel an ounce of remorse. If he hadn't arrested her and put her in this cell, she could have protected her child!

"Who took her?" she demanded, violent shudders seizing her body.

Finn's eyes clouded with despair. "I don't know. Someone came into the house, knocked Jamie unconscious and took the baby."

Air. She needed air. She couldn't breathe.

"Sarah... Lord, I'm so sorry," he whispered, each word ringing with torment. "Jamie is beyond herself—she thinks she let you down. But damn it, it wasn't her fault. The attacker gave her a nasty bump on the head...."

Sarah had already tuned him out. Her heart was beating so fast she feared her ribs might rupture. She couldn't remember the last time she'd felt this way—helpless, frightened, so completely out of control.

Someone had *taken* her baby.

The thought of Lucy at the mercy of some sadistic kidnapper brought a streak of rage to her stomach. Tears stung her eyes, then spilled over, streaming down her cheeks and soaking her chin, her neck, the front of her sweater. She heard Finn slide closer, and when he pulled her into his arms, she didn't resist, just pressed her wet face against his broad chest and cried.

"Why would someone take her?" she said between sobs. "God, Finn, she's only three months old! What if she's hungry or cold or—"

"Sarah, stop. Look at me."

His hand was on her face, cupping her chin so she had no choice but to look up at him. The agony and determination burning in his blue eyes caught her off guard. "I'm going to find her," he said in a rough voice. "I swear to you, I'll find her."

She believed him. Was she crazy for that? Everything else he'd said, his apology, his promise to help her out of this mess, his gruff declaration that he would regain her trust...she hadn't been able to bring herself to believe. But right now, she did. She *believed* he would find her daughter, even if he died trying.

Some of the terror sticking to her chest dissolved as a rush of peace floated inside of her. "Do you promise?" she whispered.

"I promise." His husky voice cracked. "I don't know who took her, or why, but I'm going to do everything in my power to get your daughter back."

The arm that had been holding her close moved up the bumps of her spine, until his hand was tangled in her hair, while his other hand drew her face to his. He bent his head, and then those lips she'd never forgotten covered hers in a kiss.

It happened so fast she didn't have time to protest, and it ended before she even could. Just the hard feel of his mouth pressed against hers, the fleeting brush of his lips, the scratch of his beard stubble against her chin.

Then he pulled back, and not giving her a chance to speak, he was on his feet and heading to the cell door. "Where are you going?" she cried after him.

His mouth was set in a straight line as he glanced over his shoulder. "I'm going to find your daughter."

She couldn't tear her eyes from the perfect, tiny creature sleeping in the crib. She'd never seen a more beautiful infant. Those impossibly long eyelashes, the cherubic cheeks and red, cupid's bow mouth. The baby's chest rose and fell at each breath she drew into her little lungs.

Emotion filled her heart, spilling over and spreading through her body.

Was this what love felt like?

The baby stirred in her sleep, sighing softly. It was physically painful to look away, but she had to make sure the changing table was stocked with all the items she'd requested. She moved across the room, smiling at the bright yellow curtains hanging on the window. She would have liked to paint the walls yellow, too, maybe put up a pretty border with clowns or balloons, but this was a log cabin, and there wasn't much she could do.

She bent down in front of the cabinet beneath the changing table, nodding in satisfaction when she saw that there were plenty of diapers, wipes, talc and anything else she might need.

A soft wail broke the peaceful silence. Lucy was awake!

She practically sprinted to the crib, eagerness soaring through her like birds taking flight. The baby had been sleeping since they'd arrived, but Lucy was up now, and she couldn't wait to hold her.

"Hi there, baby girl," she said as she reached for the drowsy-eyed infant.

Lucy blinked a couple times, then stared up at her in confusion. Another cry left her lips.

"It's okay," she whispered. "Don't cry, baby. I'm here. Mama's here."

Chapter 7

The next morning, Sarah stared absently out the window of Finn's Jeep, feeling unsettled as they drove in the direction of her house. She'd thought she'd be overjoyed to be out of that cell, that she'd throw herself on the ground and kiss the dirt, thanking God for her freedom. But the prospect of walking into her empty house and not seeing Lucy made her heart weep.

Her daughter was still missing. Despite Finn's promise that he'd bring Lucy home, he hadn't made any progress last night. She knew he'd been up all night, driving around town and knocking on doors with Max Patton and some volunteers, but they hadn't found Lucy during their search. An alert had been put out, and the media was all over the abduction—Sarah had flinched when she'd heard the radio story blare out of the speakers in Finn's Jeep.

"Woman accused of murdering Serenade resident

Teresa Donovan is in the news once again! Reports are stating her three-month-old daughter has been abducted. An Amber alert has been issued.…"

The press was eating it up, and even though it killed her to hear the things they were saying about her, she would suffer through it as long as people were looking for her daughter.

The judge had been surprisingly kind to her during the bail hearing this morning. Although he'd frowned and huffed about how he didn't like granting bail in a murder case, Sarah's distress over her missing daughter must have tugged at a couple heartstrings, because eventually he'd approved her bail, under the fervent protests of the district attorney. She'd had to put up her house as bail, and the electronic bracelet strapped around her ankle was humiliating beyond belief. But Jonas Gregory had insisted on it. Called her a flight risk.

Where exactly would she flee? she'd wanted to shout. Her daughter had been *kidnapped,* for Pete's sake. Until Lucy was safe in her arms again, she had no intention of going anywhere.

"Don't forget, you need to change the batteries every twenty-four hours," Finn spoke up, sounding extremely uncomfortable. "Otherwise the thing starts beeping."

She lifted her head. "What?"

"The ankle bracelet." He heaved out a breath. "You have to change the batteries or else it beeps and alerts the D.A. Same thing if you step out of the boundaries we programmed into it. You can't leave Serenade."

Her cheeks scorched. Was this what her life had become? A woman charged with murder, forbidden to leave town, kept on an electronic leash to make sure she stayed put. Oh, and her child was missing. How could this be happening?

She drew in a breath, forcing herself not to break apart in sobs. She had to be strong. Lucy was out there somewhere. The sweet baby she'd waited so many years for had been abducted because—because what? Why on earth would someone want to take Lucy?

In spite of her resolve, tears stung her eyes. "Why would someone take her?" she whispered.

"I don't know," Finn said gruffly. "But we'll find her, Sarah."

"You sound so sure."

"That's because the alternative is too damn horrific to contemplate."

His honesty sent a cold shiver through her body. She didn't fault him for it. Finn had always been excruciatingly blunt with her. Didn't beat around the bush, or make excuses. She'd appreciated it then.

Now...well, now, the very fact that an alternative existed—*not* finding Lucy—scared the living hell out of her.

She watched the scenery whiz by, recognizing the turnoff onto her property. The house she'd inherited from her aunt was kind of isolated, tucked behind a small forest with a gurgling creek running through it. Growing up here, away from the bustle of town, had been lonely, to say the least. But she welcomed the silence now. She wasn't sure she could face anyone in town at the moment.

God, what they must think of her. Did they believe she'd murdered Teresa Donovan? Did they think that her daughter's abduction was the perfect punishment for the crime?

"What if they took her to punish me?" she blurted out, unable to keep the frightening thought to herself.

Finn slowed the Jeep, stopping right in the middle of the dirt path leading to her house. "Nobody is punishing you," he replied firmly, reaching across the seat divider to take her hand. He squeezed it, hard, his warmth seeping into her palm and heating her frozen body. "You didn't kill Teresa, and you didn't deserve to have your daughter taken away from you."

She swallowed. "But someone else might think I'm a killer. Maybe that's why they took Lucy."

"We don't know why Lucy was taken." His jaw went stiff. "But I won't rest until we find out. You have to believe me, Sarah."

"I do," she whispered.

Looking satisfied, he moved the gearshift and drove up the driveway. Her two-story farmhouse came into view, with its slate-green roof and white exterior. Sarah was startled to see several cars parked on the dirt. She recognized Jamie's SUV and the second Jeep from the Serenade Sheriff's Department, but the two unmarked sedans were unfamiliar.

"Agent Parsons is here," Finn said, following her gaze. "And several other agents flew in this morning to help with the search for Lucy." He hesitated. "Try not to antagonize Parsons, okay? The man is a loose cannon and we can't have him getting in our way."

Nodding weakly, she unbuckled her seat belt and got out of the Jeep. Outside, the weather matched her turbulent mood. The sky was overcast, gray clouds rolling in from the east, leaving the air damp and cold. She inhaled the scent of impending rain; she'd always loved a good rainstorm. Right now, though, the cloudy sky only depressed her. She'd been stuck in that basement cell for two days, eager to get out and breathe some fresh air, but she suddenly wished she could crawl back into the dark cavern and bury her head under the covers. She couldn't face all those people inside. Parsons and the federal agents. Jamie.

Finn had said Jamie blamed herself for Lucy's abduction. He'd told her the other woman was terrified of looking into Sarah's eyes and confessing her failure to protect the child. More tears pricked her eyelids. God, she didn't blame Jamie. From what Finn had told her, the assailant had been hell-bent on getting his hands on Sarah's daughter. Jamie hadn't even had a chance to protect either of them.

To her surprise, Finn took her hand as they walked to the front porch. Two days ago, she would have shrugged out of his grip, told him she didn't want anything to do with him. She didn't do that now. Every muscle in her body vibrated with fear. She felt as if she'd been beat up, kicked, punched, thrown to the ground. Finn's touch steadied her. Soothed her.

His hand was the only thing that felt real right now.

When they entered the house, she heard voices wafting out of the large living room to the left. She fought the impulse to run upstairs and avoid the imminent questions. Or at least to shower and change—she'd been wearing these jeans and this blue turtleneck for two days already. But she couldn't dodge the inevitable. Breathing deeply, she squared her shoulders and followed Finn down the hall, knowing she'd have to face everyone sooner or later. Finn said the federal agents were anxious to speak with her about Lucy and who may have taken her, and Sarah would do anything to get her baby back, even confront Parsons and his crew.

"Sarah!"

Jamie jumped off the couch and ran toward her the second she and Finn appeared in the doorway. Sarah instinctively opened her arms, expecting Jamie to embrace her, but the auburn-haired FBI agent halted abruptly, guilt flooding her violet eyes.

"Sarah," Jamie stammered. "I'm so sorry. God, you don't know how sorry I am. He came out of nowhere, hit me before I could—"

Sarah took the other woman into her arms before Jamie could even finish. After a moment of stiffness, Jamie hugged her back, her slender frame shaking. "It wasn't your fault," Sarah said, fighting another rush of tears. "I know you did everything you could to protect Lucy."

Jamie pulled away with an impassioned look in her eyes. "I'm going to get her back for you. I won't give up until we find her."

"Ms. Connelly?"

Sarah turned to the four people in black suits staring expectantly at her. Parsons was standing by the window, a slight frown on his face. The other three were on the couch, two men and a woman, each one sporting a grave expression as they introduced themselves to her. Several coffee cups sat on the long wood coffee table, all filled to the rim, obviously untouched. Finn had given Jamie the key to Sarah's house and asked her to wait with the federal agents, but apparently the Bureau's people weren't interested in coffee or pleasantries.

And they got right down to business after Sarah settled on an armchair across from the couch.

"Do you have any idea who might have kidnapped the child?"

"Do you have any enemies we need to be aware of?"

"Is the father in the picture?"

The questions flew from their mouths like shells from a shotgun. Rubbing the bridge of her nose, Sarah let out a breath, then focused on the first question, posed to her by one of the males, Agent Bradley. With a head of thick black hair and kind brown eyes, he looked far warmer than Mark Parsons.

"I have no idea who might have taken her," she said softly. She turned to the Agent Andrews, a petite blonde with freckles. "And I don't have any enemies. None that I know of, anyway."

"And the child's father?" the third, Agent Ferraro, prompted. Now *he* reminded her of Parsons—he had that same shrewd glint in his eyes.

"I don't know who the father is," she confessed. "I adopted Lucy three months ago, through an agency in Raleigh. Her original birth certificate wasn't in the file—apparently, the birth mother wanted to remain anonymous and the head of the agency said she hadn't listed a father. They issued a new certificate for me, naming me as her mother, with the father unknown."

"Do you have records of the adoption?" Parsons drawled from the window.

Her spine stiffened. What the hell did he think, that she'd kidnapped Lucy herself? "Of course I do," she replied in a frigid tone.

He offered a cheerless smile. "We'll need to see those."

"And pictures," Agent Andrews spoke up, sympathy glimmering in her eyes as she turned to Sarah. "We'll need the most recent photographs of the child."

Sarah was already standing up. "I have everything in my study. I'll go get it."

"I'll join you," came Parsons's snide voice.

She tried to hide her lack of enthusiasm. She got the feeling he was coming along to keep an eye on her, make sure she didn't try to shred the documents or something. Finn trailed after her, too, the annoyed look on his handsome face telling her he wasn't happy with Parsons, either.

The study she used was on the second floor, three doors down from her bedroom. The spacious room consisted of a walnut desk that held her desktop computer, several filing cabinets she used for her business, and a bookshelf crammed with paperbacks and art books. Moving toward the tallest filing cabinet, she bent down and opened the bottom drawer, flipping through folders until she found the one she was looking for.

She stood up and held out the folder to Parsons, who was watching her with narrowed eyes.

"It's all there," she said, cringing at the defensive note in her voice. "The records from the adoption agency, Lucy's birth certificate, her medical records." She swallowed. "Her entire life is in there."

What life? Lucy was three months old. God, her daughter hadn't even lived yet. And now...now she was gone, and who knew what the person who took her was doing to her.

Suddenly feeling weak, Sarah sagged against one of the cabinets, fighting to collect her composure.

"Sarah," came Finn's rough voice. "Maybe you should sit down."

"I...I'm fine." She took a calming breath. "I just had a moment of panic."

Parsons moved his head back and forth between them, narrowing his eyes even more.

"What?" Sarah finally snapped. "Why are you looking at me like that?"

"Just pondering, that's all." He tilted his head, a lock of blond hair falling onto his forehead. "Where's your daughter, Ms. Connelly?"

She stared at him in bewilderment. "What?"

He moved closer, a patronizing light in his eyes. "Do you know where she is?"

"Why would I—" She stopped, her spine going rigid. "You think I had something to do with this."

When he didn't answer, an eddy of anger swirled in her belly, joined by a rush of disbelief. How could anyone possibly think she'd had anything to do with her daughter's abduction?

"You son of a bitch," Finn muttered, taking a step toward the agent. "Are you accusing Sarah of kidnapping her own daughter?"

"Just looking at every angle," Parsons replied, unfazed. "In the majority of child abductions, a family member is usually the culprit."

Sarah bit back a growl. "Do I have to remind you that I was in *jail* when my baby was taken?"

He shrugged. "Perhaps you had someone on the outside helping you." He shot Finn a pointed look.

Sarah balled her hands into fists. "I cannot believe you're even suggesting this! I did *not* arrange for my child to be abducted!"

Parsons edged off to the side, as if he thought she was going to pounce on him—which she was seriously tempted to do. Taking a long breath, Sarah forced her feet to stay rooted to the floor. She could only imagine what her face looked like right now—wild eyes, tight features. She had to calm down. Parsons already thought she was a murderer. She refused to give him any more ammunition against her.

Exhaling slowly, she met the man's eyes. "I have no

idea where my daughter is, Agent Parsons, and I suggest you stop interrogating me about it and go out and do your job."

Parsons frowned. He looked ready to say something nasty, but Finn spoke up before he could open his mouth. "Sarah, can you find those pictures?"

She held Parsons's gaze for another second, then gave a brief nod. Turning away, she headed to the bookshelf and grabbed a red leather photo album from one of the shelves. Fortunately, she'd developed a ton of digital prints only three days before she'd been arrested. She flipped through the pages to find suitable photos, her heart jamming in her throat as Lucy's angelic face stared up at her.

Her hands started to tremble. Each photo sent a hot blade of agony to her chest. Lucy sleeping in her crib. Lucy lying on her back, kicking her little feet in the air as she stared at the lens. Lucy smiling her adorable toothless smile.

Battling the pain shooting through her, she selected three of the most recent pictures and silently handed them to Parsons. He tucked them into the file folder she'd given him, then exited the study without a word, leaving her and Finn alone.

Sarah looked down at the open photo album in her shaky hands, then met Finn's surprisingly gentle eyes. "She's gone, Finn. My baby's gone."

He moved toward her, his stride long and quick. A second later, she was in his arms, her face pressed against his collarbone, the album still in her hands, crushed between them. She felt his heartbeat hammering against her breasts, matching the frantic pounding of her own pulse.

Running his hands over her lower back, he held her

tight and murmured, "You're not alone, Sarah. I'm here for you."

All his words did was bring another jolt of pain to her heart. Yes, he was here, and yes, his comforting embrace was so achingly familiar she wanted to cry again. But that didn't mean she wanted to rely on him. Lean on him. This man had hurt her. He'd abandoned her. He was the last person she should be seeking comfort from.

Regaining her senses, she slowly moved out of his arms and rubbed her tired eyes. "I'd rather Lucy was here," she whispered.

A cloud of torment darkened his eyes. She knew she'd hurt him by saying that, but she couldn't stop the resentment suddenly lodged in her chest. He was here. Now. But what about before? What about when she'd needed him *then?*

"Sheriff, I'd like it if you joined us," came Parsons's voice, the sharp order drifting in from the other room.

Finn swallowed. "I…we should go back out there."

She avoided his gaze. "Can you give me a minute? I just…" Her eyes dropped to the photo album. "I just need a minute."

He nodded. "Come when you're ready."

And then he was gone, and Sarah let out a breath, walking on numb legs toward the desk chair. She sank down, still holding the album. She opened it to the last few pages, which contained the pictures she'd taken only last week by the circular fountain in the town square. Martha, the owner of the diner, had been walking by, and Sarah had asked the older woman to take a few shots of her and Lucy.

In one, Sarah had her arms up high, Lucy dangling from above, while Sarah gazed up at the child in adoration. The next one featured Lucy on her lap, her chubby hands reaching to snag a lock of Sarah's hair. Lucy loved tugging on her hair. It hurt sometimes, but she always indulged her daughter, who was so sweet, so curious and sunny and—*gone*.

God, Lucy was gone.

The sound of quiet footsteps had her lifting her head, just as Finn's deputy, Max Patton, appeared in the doorway. Apprehension lined his brown eyes and the slouch of his shoulders made him appear younger. She'd always thought Max was a cute guy, with his floppy brown hair and dimpled cheeks. And he was unfailingly nice to her when they ran into each other in town.

Right now, though, she didn't want him here. She didn't want anyone. Only Lucy.

"Ms. Connelly," Max started, shifting awkwardly, "I just wanted to tell you how sorry I am about your baby."

Her throat clogged. "I appreciate that, Max."

"I mean it," he went on. "I can't even imagine what you're going through right now, but I assure you, we're doing everything we can to get Lucy back."

"Thank you," she murmured.

He hesitated in the doorway for a few more seconds, then gave her a sad smile and disappeared, leaving her to her photographs.

The last one Martha had taken that day hurt the most to look at. Lucy was smiling. Not just smiling, but *beaming*. Looking at Sarah with sheer, unconditional love in her big, perceptive eyes.

"I can't lose you," Sarah whispered, running her thumb over Lucy's tiny face. "I can't do this again."

She tipped her head, her gaze moving to the ceiling

as agony seized her stomach and tore her insides apart. "Don't make me go through this again," she begged, hoping someone was listening to her.

Perhaps the higher power that hadn't listened before.

"Please," she whispered. "Please don't do this to me again."

After the federal agents finally cleared out of Sarah's house, Finn released a breath heavy with relief. Lord, he couldn't stand this. There was nothing worse than a child going missing. Not knowing if she was safe. If she was cold or hungry or suffering. He didn't even blame Sarah for hiding away in the study. She hadn't come out since the confrontation with Parsons, and Finn hadn't had the heart to drag her back into the midst.

There was nothing she could do, anyway. Except wait.

And pray.

"I hope one of those leads pans out," Jamie murmured as she stood in the hallway, wringing her hands together.

It took him a moment to remember what she was talking about. Right, the leads. Anna had just phoned from the station, informing him that a dozen calls had come in from people claiming to have seen Lucy, or insisting they had information about the abduction. That's why the FBI agents had hightailed it out of here, to follow-up on the incoming stream of tips.

But Finn wasn't convinced the so-called leads would amount to anything. He'd never handled a kidnapping before, but he knew from other law enforcement colleagues just how many false alarms came in during these types of cases. With the media putting a spotlight on the abduction, attention-hungry lowlifes crept from the gutters, hoping to get their fifteen minutes of fame.

Maybe this time, though... He prayed that this time one of those phone calls actually led to Lucy's safe return.

"I should get going," Jamie said, sounding reluctant. "Cole's probably pacing the house, going crazy that he can't help. He called his investigator, though, so we've got another person on board, determined to find Lucy."

"Thank Cole when you see him." Finn was about to offer to pay the P.I.'s tab, then thought twice. Cole Donovan was a millionaire, for chrissake. He probably had a whole slew of investigators on retainer.

"Give Sarah a hug for me," Jamie said as she left.

Finn closed the door after her, then turned to Max, who was leaning against the wall in the corridor. "What now, boss?" Max asked.

Finn sighed. "Now you go back to the station and help Anna field calls. I'll stay here and keep an eye on Sarah."

"You got it, Sheriff."

Once Max was gone, Finn headed upstairs, a bit fearful of what he'd find when he entered the study. He still couldn't believe Parsons had had the gall to accuse Sarah of arranging to kidnap her own child. Jamie was right—that jerk had tunnel vision, and right now, his narrow sights were set on Sarah.

But Finn knew better. He would never forget the day Sarah came back to Serenade, after spending a month in Raleigh awaiting the birth of her daughter. He'd been coming out of the diner just as she walked in with Lucy on her hip, and the joy he'd seen in her eyes had been so strong and all-consuming he was surprised it hadn't infected the rest of the town. She loved that baby. He'd been overwhelmed by the force of that love, the tenderness as she'd introduced him to Lucy.

In that moment, their rocky past had ceased to exist. Sarah had been so wrapped up in the child, swept away by a wave of maternal love, that she'd forgotten everything. She'd even smiled at him.

No way was she faking any of this. If she'd had someone take Lucy, that meant her pain, her terror, was all make-believe. And nobody was that good of an actor.

He reached the study, took a breath, and knocked. There was no answer.

"Sarah?" he said cautiously. "Can I come in?"

Silence.

Sighing, he pushed open the door, expecting to find her curled up in the corner of the room, crying over the photo album, but the study was empty. With a frown, he strode out, heading down the hall toward Sarah's bedroom. The door was ajar, and when he walked in, he found that empty, too.

His pulse sped up. Where the hell was she?

He checked the bathroom next, the guest rooms, and after he'd searched the second floor twice, he raced down the stairs, panic blowing around in his gut like street litter. Every room he peered in was deserted. No Sarah. She was gone.

"Damn it," he mumbled to himself.

She'd taken off. Must have sneaked out while everyone had been in the living room, discussing her *missing daughter*. Was Parsons right? Had Sarah somehow been involved in— He halted in the hallway. The ankle bracelet. There was a GPS in it, and both he and the D.A. had a unit that could monitor Sarah's movements.

As anger and frustration boiled inside of him, he

raced outside and flung open the back door of the Jeep, grabbing the duffel bag he'd left in the backseat. He unzipped it and rummaged around until he found the GPS locator. It was the size of a BlackBerry, with a screen that displayed a map featuring a red dot.

The dot wasn't moving.

He peered at the screen, then felt the blood drain from his face. He recognized the location on the map. It was less than a mile from here and the red blip remained static, indicating that Sarah was staying put. He knew why she'd gone there. Hell, it should have been the first place he'd thought to look.

A headache formed between his eyes. Gulping hard, he reached up to rub away the ache, then unclipped his car keys from his belt and slid into the driver's seat of the Jeep.

God, Sarah, why did you have to go there?

It was hard to drive in the condition he was in. Along with the throbbing temples, his heart thudded erratically in his chest, each beat sending a streak of grief through him. He couldn't do this, he realized as he steered the Jeep toward the turnoff. He couldn't do this. He hadn't been there in years.

Three minutes later, the wrought-iron gates came into view, and his pulse sped up even more. His mouth was totally dry. He couldn't swallow. He couldn't even park the car; his hands were shaking that badly.

Sucking in a burst of oxygen, he forced himself to calm down. Sarah was here, right beyond those gates. He might not want to walk through them, but he had no choice. Steadying his hands, he parked in the tiny gravel lot next to the gate and staggered out of the vehicle.

"You can do this," he muttered to himself.

Christ, could he?

The metal creaked as he parted the heavy gates and stepped onto the damp grass beyond the entrance. He made a conscious effort not to look around. Look straight ahead. Walk deeper into the cemetery. He was just climbing a gentle grassy slope when the rain began to fall and cool droplets stained his face. He wiped them away, reaching the top of the slope. He took a breath, then turned his head to the right, knowing exactly what he'd find.

And there she was, on her knees, huddled by a simple, blue-granite tombstone, her thick brown hair blown around by the wet breeze.

You can do this.

His legs shook with each step he took, but he soldiered on, getting closer. Closer. Until he was directly behind her. Until his suddenly moist eyes honed in on the headstone that Sarah was kneeling in front of, the headstone that had her shuddering with silent sobs.

Jason Finnegan

Beloved son of Patrick and Sarah.
Here for a short time, but forever in our hearts.

Chapter 8

Sarah whirled around as she heard footsteps from behind. She quickly swiped her sleeve over her wet eyes, then dropped her arm when she saw it was Finn. No point hiding her tears from him. He knew better than anyone what she was going through right now.

As he moved closer, the wind plastered his dark blue Windbreaker against his chest and raindrops slid down his proud forehead. He looked incredibly handsome, and incredibly sad. She suddenly remembered the day of the funeral, the way he'd looked in his black suit and tie, with the hair he'd neglected to cut for months curling under his chin and shining in the morning sunlight. That was when their relationship had begun to deteriorate.

No, that wasn't true, she realized. It happened after she'd discovered she was pregnant with Jason. *That's* when everything had changed.

"You shouldn't have run off like that without telling anyone," Finn said roughly, shoving his hands in the pockets of his jeans.

"I'm sorry," she said, and meant it. "I just... I couldn't sit there anymore. It was too quiet."

He didn't answer. From the corner of her eye, she saw that his gaze was focused on the tiny headstone. The grief slashing across his rugged features made her breathless. At the funeral he'd donned a shuttered expression, stood there in stoic silence. A part of her had wondered if he even cared about the loss of their son.

She slowly stood up, ignoring the grass stains on her denim-clad knees. Wrapping her arms around her chest, she turned to Finn, tears shimmering in her eyes and blurring her vision. "You didn't want him," she found herself whispering.

His jaw tensed for a second, then relaxed, a cloud of defeat moving across his face. "Not at first," he said hoarsely.

No, he definitely hadn't been pleased when she'd told him about the pregnancy. It hadn't been planned—she'd been twenty-three at the time, Finn only twenty-six. Neither of them had wanted a baby, not then, but although Sarah was surprised, she'd quickly adjusted to the pregnancy. Jason might have been an accident, but she'd loved him from the second she knew he existed.

Not Finn, though. She cringed as she remembered his shocked reaction. They'd been having breakfast in the kitchen of his farmhouse, where they'd lived for nearly a year. At first, he hadn't even reacted, hadn't even blinked.

And then he'd asked her if she wanted to terminate the pregnancy.

She hadn't wanted to, but in that moment, she'd realized that *he* did.

"I was always up-front with you about it," Finn said, his husky voice bringing her back to the present. "I never wanted children. I never wanted to be a husband or father."

She bristled. "It's not like I got pregnant on purpose."

"I know you didn't. But I still wasn't pleased about it," he confessed. "And then, when you told me you were keeping the baby, I let myself, I don't know, *hope*. I hoped that maybe everything would work out. That maybe my mother hadn't messed me up as bad as I thought and I could truly be the man you wanted me to be."

Sarah held her breath. He'd never said any of this to her before. A part of her wondered if he even realized what he was doing. His blue eyes were fixed on that little grave, his voice sounding faraway to her ears.

"Seeing you carrying him…watching your belly swell…feeling him kick against my palm." Finn let out a choked sound, his despair echoing in the air, mingling with the soft spattering of raindrops against the grass. "I *wanted* him, Sarah. I wanted him so damn badly it hurt to look at you."

As her heart pounded in her chest, she took a step toward him and reached up to touch the stubble coating his jaw. "Why didn't you ever tell me this before?"

"I couldn't," he blurted out. "When we went to the doctor and saw that ultrasound…when he told us that Jason was…"

To her shock, tears filled his eyes. In all the years she'd known him, she'd never once seen him cry. He certainly hadn't cried during the doctor's visit he was describing, yet she now realized he'd been just as affected that day.

Back then, she'd believed he was relieved by the news. It was the only way to explain his lack of…lack of *everything.*

I'm sorry, but your baby's gone.

At eight-and-a-half-months pregnant, finding out her child died in utero had been like dying herself. Sarah had felt as though someone had taken a baseball bat and pounded the living hell out of her. She'd sat there, numb, paralyzed, as the doctor threw out words like stillborn and undiagnosed preeclampsia and needing to induce labor.

And the entire time, Finn hadn't said a word. He hadn't comforted her. Held her. Brushed away her tears. He'd simply shut down, leaving her to battle the grief and shock all by herself.

"I wanted to die that day," Finn said in a ravaged voice. "I kept asking myself if maybe it was my fault. If maybe God was punishing me for not wanting Jason when you first told me about him."

His heart-wrenching words brought tears to her eyes. Without stopping to think about what she was doing, she wrapped her arms around his neck and held him with everything she had. She felt his sorrow and shame vibrating from his body, his heartbeat thudding irregularly against her chest.

"God, Sarah, I blamed myself for what happened," he whispered, his breath fanning over the top of her head. "And then you fell apart, and I couldn't think straight. I'd already been through all that with my mother, all the memories just reared their ugly heads, and I couldn't be there for you. I just couldn't."

His arms tightened around her and she nearly

drowned in his strong embrace. "You never told me you blamed yourself," she said, tipping her head up to meet his tormented gaze.

"You were going through a tough time. I didn't want to drop my own issues on you and make it worse."

Her heart constricted, sending a jolt of pain through her body. Why hadn't he said this to her four years ago? Why had he let her face the depression alone, pretending he didn't give a damn about the son they'd lost? She pressed her cheek into his neck, breathing in the familiar scent of him, spicy, masculine, soothing.

She didn't know how long they stood there, holding each other as the rain gently fell over them, but when they finally pulled apart, something changed between them. Something shifted inside her.

"Come on," Finn said, reaching for her hand. "I'll take you home."

Finn felt as though he'd run a marathon followed by two triathlons as he trailed upstairs after Sarah. They'd returned to her house just as the rain became a downpour, and they'd both been drenched during the walk from the car to the porch. He was chilled to the bone, though he suspected it had more to do with his graveyard confession than the rain.

When he'd found Sarah kneeling in front of their son's grave, something had broken inside of him. For four years, he'd tried desperately to block out any thoughts of Jason, to pretend that the loss had been for the best. He hadn't wanted to be a father, hadn't wanted to settle down. That's what he'd told himself whenever the memory of his tiny son breached the shield he'd constructed around himself.

But the lies he'd clung to had unraveled like an old

sweater back at the cemetery. He'd loved his son. Loved him in a fierce, protective way that only a father could feel.

Why hadn't he been there for Sarah? She'd been suffering just as much as he was, if not more so, and instead of sharing her pain, he'd abandoned her. But it had been too much for him. Growing up with a bipolar mother had been difficult, especially since his mom refused to take her meds most of the time. He'd been a caretaker for his entire childhood and adolescence, and when his mother committed suicide when Finn was eighteen, he'd felt such overwhelming relief it still shamed him to remember it. He'd finally been free of his responsibilities, able to live his life without worrying about cleaning up other people's messes.

He hadn't lied to Sarah—he *didn't* want to settle down, or be a husband, have kids. All he'd wanted was his independence, and an unplanned pregnancy hadn't meshed with the life he'd envisioned for himself. That changed, though, when he felt Jason kick for the first time. At that moment, feeling the little flutter against his hand, he'd vowed to be the best father and husband he could be.

And then Jason had died, and Finn had not only destroyed Sarah, but himself.

"Why don't you hop in the shower and I'll throw your clothes in the dryer?" Sarah offered.

He was about to refuse, but the wet denim clinging to his legs made him reconsider. "Sure. That sounds good."

She led him to the door across from her bedroom. "You can shower here. Just leave the clothes on the bed."

His mouth went dry as he wondered whether she

planned to stick around and watch him undress. Disappointment flickered inside of him when she moved to the door, saying, "I'll give you some privacy."

Sighing, Finn sat on the bed and unlaced his boots. He kicked them off, peeled away his socks, then tackled his wet clothes. He strode naked into the bathroom, where he plucked a towel from the rack and wrapped it around his waist before going to gather up his clothing. He was just laying them on the bed when a tentative knock sounded.

"You decent?" Sarah called. "I just wanted to get those clothes."

"Yeah, come in."

She strode through the doorway, then froze when she caught sight of him. He glimpsed a brief flicker of heat, and it made him want to flex his muscles or some ridiculous crap, just to see those liquid brown eyes smolder. Her gaze swept over his bare chest, causing hot shivers to travel along his skin. His groin tightened, an erection growing beneath the towel around his hip. He shifted, hoping she wouldn't notice, but her sensual lips parted slightly, confirming she'd seen everything.

His arousal was so wrong, on so many levels. Not only had they just returned from a visit to the cemetery, but Sarah's daughter was still missing. He wasn't allowed to be turned-on right now, though in his defense, turned-on wasn't an uncommon state for him when Sarah was around.

Breaking eye contact, he took a step back, determined to control his body's response to her proximity. Hop in the shower, get dressed, offer to make her some lunch. That's what he needed to do right now.

But Sarah had other ideas.

His mouth went bone-dry as she moved closer, an

undecipherable expression in her eyes. Holding his breath, he waited to see what she would do. What she would say.

She'd changed into a tight green sweater and a pair of snug jeans before taking off to the cemetery, and the material was now soaked from the rain, clinging to her slender frame and displaying the curvy contours of her body like a damn Thanksgiving feast. Her nipples were puckered, poking against one of those paper-thin bras she'd always liked to wear. His pulse raced as he remembered those dusky-pink nubs, the way they went even more rigid when he captured them between his lips.

"Finn," she began, her voice ringing with anguish.

Before he could say a word, she had her arms twined around his neck, up on her tiptoes as she kissed him. Her mouth was desperate, moving over his in a frantic kiss, and then her tongue probed at the seam of his lips, demanding entry.

He couldn't do anything but let her in. His body went taut with anticipation, his erection thickening as she explored his mouth with her tongue and dug her fingernails into the nape of his neck.

He utilized every ounce of willpower to break the kiss. His voice came out in a ragged burst of air. "What are you doing?"

"Forgetting," she whispered, and then she kissed him again.

Somehow they moved to the bed. Somehow his hands found their way underneath her sweater, sliding up to cup her firm breasts over her lacy bra. Pure, unadulterated desire crashed into him. He squeezed her breasts, then yanked the sweater up and her bra down, and rubbed his cheek against the swollen mounds.

He covered one nipple with his mouth, suckling gently, eliciting a moan from her lips. He laved her with his tongue, nipped at her with his teeth, as wave after wave of sheer exhilaration crashed over him. Lord, he was kissing Sarah. Touching Sarah. He'd been dreaming about this for four years and as she suddenly pushed him onto his back and straddled his thighs, he realized that nothing had changed. He was harder than he'd ever been in his life, his pulse was pounding so loudly he couldn't hear a thing. She'd always done this to him, made him hot and dizzy and hungry for her. So damn hungry.

Something has *changed.*

The notion slipped into his hazy mind, pushing through the passion and arousal and uncontrollable need. With a low groan, he gripped her waist and stilled her, putting an end to the seductive roll of her lower body against his aching groin. He looked into her eyes and saw the dazed expression there, the desperation.

She didn't want him.

She just wanted to *forget.*

"Why are you stopping?" she murmured, leaning down to kiss him again.

Maybe he was the biggest idiot on the planet, but he turned his head, so that her soft lips collided with his cheek. It was physically painful to move, but he did it anyway, sliding out from under her and stumbling off the bed. Breathing heavily, he stared into her confused eyes and said, "I can't do this."

"Why not?" Biting her lip she glanced at his crotch. "I can see you want me. Don't tell me it's not true."

"I do want you," he squeezed out. "I've wanted you for four years. I've fantasized about this happening, sweetheart, so many times." His lungs burned as he inhaled deeply. "But it can't be like this. It can't be about grief, or sorrow, or you needing to forget about Jason and Lucy and this damn murder case."

Her shoulders sagged. "Maybe it's not about that."

"It is," he corrected. "It's all about forgetting."

"So?" Irritation flashed in her eyes. "Does it really matter what it's about?"

"It does to me." A lump rose in the back of his throat. "You have to want me. *Me,* Sarah. When we make love, it needs to be because you want to be with me, fully, not just to forget about everything else."

She didn't answer, and he didn't push her. She knew he was right, he could see it on her face, in that helpless, frustrated crease lining her forehead. It made his entire body ache, how damn beautiful she was. All that creamy, flawless skin, her lush cupid's bow mouth, the damp hair curling at the ends. He wanted to take back everything he'd just said, cover her body with his and lose himself inside her.

Fortunately, his phone started to ring before he could act on that foolish urge.

Turning away, he picked up the cell phone from the top of the dresser, frowning when he saw Parsons's number on the screen.

"Finnegan," he barked into the phone.

"Sheriff, it's Parsons. We may have a lead on the child."

Finn sucked in a breath. "Tell me."

"One of my agents just handled a tip from a woman who owns a baby boutique in Grayden." For once, Parsons sounded concerned rather than smug. "She heard about Lucy's abduction on the news and said she might have information. Apparently, a woman came into the boutique six days ago, looking, and I quote, 'extremely agitated.'"

Finn's instincts started buzzing. "Agitated?"

"Yeah. The owner says the customer was acting really weird and nervous. She tried making conversation with her, asking who the baby clothes were for, but the customer got even more pale. She refused to answer any questions, ended up buying a whole bunch of stuff and pretty much sprinted from the shop."

A mysterious woman purchasing baby garments and refusing to talk about it? Running out the door? Oh, yeah, for once in his sorry life, Parsons was actually on to something.

"We need to find this woman," Finn said. "Whoever she is—"

"We already found her."

He nearly dropped the phone. "What?"

"I sent Andrews and Ferraro to the boutique an hour ago. Andrews just phoned in." Parsons hesitated. "The owner showed them the security footage from the day in question. Both my agents immediately recognized the customer."

Unease washed over him. "Who was it, Parsons?"

"Anna Holt. Your deputy."

Chapter 9

"Anna wouldn't do this," Sarah said firmly, shaking her head in dismay as they entered the police station twenty minutes later.

Finn was too wired up to respond. Ever since Parsons's phone call, his head had been spinning. Like Sarah, he didn't believe that Anna was involved in Lucy's abduction, but he couldn't ignore the evidence, either. A nervous-looking Anna had been spotted buying baby clothes at a shop in the next town over.

Why hadn't she gone to the maternity store in Serenade? Why drive thirty minutes to another town? And why buy baby clothing to begin with? Anna was twenty-four years old, single, still living with her parents. What reason did she have to purchase baby stuff?

It didn't make sense to him, and as they entered the bull pen, he prayed there was another explanation for that security footage. Only problem was, Anna was out with the volunteer unit, knocking on doors and asking questions about the kidnapping. Parsons had been hell-bent on tracking her down and dragging her back to the police station, but Finn had ordered the agent not to make a single move until he got there. He had promptly thrown back on his damp clothes, forgoing the shower, then waited for Sarah to quickly change into something dry. They were out of the house in a flash, neither of them bringing up the passionate encounter in the guest room.

He would bring it up, though. Not now. Later. When they cleared up this latest mess. When they found Lucy.

Parsons and the three other federal agents were waiting in the bull pen, drinking coffee and talking among themselves. When Parsons saw Finn, he stood up and said, "Why are you all wet?"

"It's raining outside, in case you haven't noticed." Finn headed for his office, over his shoulder adding, "Give me two minutes. I need to change into some dry clothes."

In his office, he opened the metal locker near the door, ignoring the olive-green sheriff's uniform neatly hanging inside. He never wore the uniform—it was too stiff and uncomfortable. Instead, he grabbed a spare pair of jeans and a gray hooded sweatshirt, then stripped off his wet attire and got dressed. When he strode back into the bull pen a minute later, Parsons was still on his feet, arms crossed as he said, "We need to bring Deputy Holt in, Sheriff."

"We can't, not unless we want to spook her," Finn retorted. He escorted Sarah to the chair in front of Max's station, then leaned against the desk. "If she has the baby, and I'm not certain she does, then she might bolt if she thinks we're on to her."

Parsons's mouth tightened in a thin line. "What do you suggest, then?"

"We wait for her to come back." Finn glanced at the clock hanging over the coffee station. "It's three o'clock. Anna went out with the volunteer unit around noon. I'll call her and say I need her here at the station, but we're not going to turn on the sirens and go after her. If she does have Lucy and thinks we know it, she might disappear."

Parsons offered a resigned nod. "You're right. We need to play it safe. We don't want her running off."

Finn was surprised the other man gave in so easily, but even Parsons had to see the validity of Finn's point. Not that he thought Anna abducted the baby. This had to be a misunderstanding.

"Do you have a copy of the security footage from the boutique?" Finn asked.

Andrews, the pretty female agent, nodded and gestured to the laptop in front of her. "I just downloaded it. Come and take a look."

Both Finn and Sarah approached the screen, and three minutes later, they wore identical frowns. It was no mistake. Anna was the woman on the tape, and just as Parsons had described, she'd looked pale, nervous and extremely jumpy during the encounter at the baby store.

Rubbing his chin in frustration, Finn edged away from the laptop. Sarah did, too, sinking back in Max's chair as she said, "They were blue."

Everyone turned in her direction.

"The clothes," she clarified. "They were blue, like she was buying them for a boy."

"Possibly to throw off suspicion," Agent Andrews suggested. "She obviously didn't want to advertise she was planning on abducting a child. Anything pink might have raised suspicion once it came out that a baby girl had been taken."

Sarah gave a little sigh, an acknowledgment that Andrews had a point.

"Look," Finn began, "just because she was at the store doesn't mean that—"

"Uh...hi. What's going on?"

Finn swiveled his head, smothering a groan when he saw Max in the doorway. His deputy took one look around the room, picked up on the tension hanging in the air, and clumsily repeated his question. "Seriously, what's up?"

"Just discussing a new lead," Finn said vaguely.

A thought suddenly occurred to him. Max and Anna were about the same age, and Finn knew for a fact they went out for drinks together on their nights off. He wasn't sure whether they were dating—he didn't think so—but he did know they were close. If anyone might be able to help him gain insight about Anna, it was Max.

Excusing himself, Finn moved away from the group and headed toward the bewildered man across the room. He lightly touched Max's elbow. "Can I speak to you alone for a second?"

Still looking confused, Max nodded. "Sure, boss."

They headed out into the hall, where Finn got right to the point. "Listen...this might sound odd, but...you're close with Anna, right?"

Max furrowed his eyebrows. "Yeah, we're good friends."

"That's what I thought." Finn chose his next words carefully. "Is there any reason why Anna would buy baby clothes?"

The deputy seemed startled. "Baby clothes? I don't think she would, especially since—" He stopped abruptly.

Finn's hackles rose. "Since what?"

His deputy glanced at the floor. "Nothing. Forget I said anything."

"Max. What do you know?"

"Sir, this is kind of personal. I'd really rather not—"

"Max." Finn tamped down his frustration. "Why would Anna not have a need for baby clothes?"

A sigh left Max's mouth. "Because she can't have children."

Finn's stomach dropped like a lead weight. "What?"

"She was in a really bad car accident when she was fourteen," Max confessed, looking uncomfortable. "She broke her pelvis, and there was a bunch of other damage, and the doctors had to remove her...you know, do a hysterectomy."

Oh, Christ. Along with the sympathy that flooded him at the notion that Anna couldn't have kids, the knowledge also made him want to curse. Only a short while ago, he'd seen a segment on the news about a barren woman who'd abducted an infant from a hospital nursery in order to satisfy her desperate need to be a mother. What if Anna had done the same thing? What if she'd wanted a baby so badly she'd decided to steal one?

No, that was ridiculous. He'd always prided himself on being a good judge of character. Anna Holt was a first-class woman. Kind, intelligent, with a truly good heart.

"Boss, I really don't understand why—" Max's mouth fell open. "Sheriff, you don't actually think *Anna* had something to do with any of this."

"With any of what?" came a wary female voice.

Both men spun around to find Anna standing at the end of the corridor. In her green deputy's uniform, with her dark hair tied back in a low ponytail, she looked young and professional. Her strides were quick as she moved toward them, her normally astute eyes flickering with suspicion.

"What's going on?" she asked. Her voice cracked. "What's happening?"

Finn swallowed the sigh lodged in his chest. He hated that he had to do this. He'd rather cut off his own arm than cause this young woman any pain. She trusted him. Respected him. And if they were wrong here...

And if she has Lucy?

He heeded the firm reminder. Lucy was the only one that mattered right now, and if Anna knew anything about the baby's kidnapping, Finn needed to get that information out of her. If she didn't...well, maybe her trust and respect were the price he'd have to pay.

"Anna," he said gently, "I'm going to need you to come with me."

"I did *not* kidnap that baby," Anna exclaimed fifteen minutes later, her dark eyes filling with tears. She turned to Finn in accusation. "How could you even *think* that, Sheriff? How *could* you?"

Finn's heart rolled painfully in his chest. In the four years of serving as Serenade's sheriff, he'd learned how to distance himself during interrogations. It was hard to do, especially when the person sitting across the table was someone you knew well, someone you saw around town and had coffee with in the diner. But he'd always made a heroic effort to keep that distance, to treat each matter objectively and get past the fact that sometimes people he called friends might need to be punished.

But this was unbelievably difficult. This was Anna, for Pete's sake.

After he'd shown her the security tape, he'd let Parsons take over the questioning, mostly because he couldn't even look at his young deputy without wanting to clock himself in the face. As Parsons made the reason for this chat clear, Anna's confusion and wariness had transformed into outrage that palpitated in the room.

"Then why did you buy baby clothes in Grayden?" Parsons demanded.

"It…they were for my cousin," she sputtered. "Linda. She lives in Charlotte and just gave birth to a baby boy. His name is James." Anna's tears spilled over, two rivers of misery that rippled down her cheeks. "You can ask my parents. They'll tell you it's true."

Parsons looked unaffected by her obvious distress. "We've seen the tape, Deputy Holt. You look like a nervous bunny rabbit on it. The owner of the store said you refused to talk about the purchase."

"Because it hurt!"

The outburst had Finn's insides clenching. There was no mistaking the agony ringing from her voice, and in that moment, he realized that this really was a mistake. Anna's actions, now that he'd learned of her infertility from Max, made a hell of a lot more sense.

"I can't have children, okay?" she cried. "Maybe one day I'll adopt, the way Ms. Connelly did, but that doesn't mean I'm fine with it. When I see a baby, it still makes me sad. And when my cousin, who's the exact same age as me, just gives birth to a beautiful little boy…"

She let out a shaky breath. "I was buying those things for James, and the entire time I was in the store, I just wanted to run from there. I don't care if that makes me a coward, but it *hurt*."

She finished in a rush, leaving both men slightly stunned. Finn's throat was so tight he could barely speak, but he managed a quick nod at Parsons, who slowly pushed back his chair.

"We'll be right back," Finn said, unable to meet Anna's eyes.

In the hall, Parsons crossed his arms, but the look in his eyes told Finn that the federal agent was on the same page. "She didn't do it," Finn murmured.

"Yeah, I don't think so, either."

"We need to let her go."

This time Parsons disagreed. "If we do, I'm assigning Ferraro to keep an eye on her. She might have been quite convincing in there, but we can't take any chances, Finnegan. She might still lead us to that baby."

"I don't think she will."

Parsons's nostrils flared. "I don't care what you think. You might be leading the Donovan murder, but I was assigned to the abduction. If I think Holt merits more attention, you can't do a damn thing about it."

Finn tried not to sigh. So much for Parsons's transformation. The man was the same controlling jerk.

"Fine," he finally muttered. "Do whatever you want."

"Gee, thanks for the permission," Parsons said in a cutting voice. "Now I'm going to talk to Ferraro about his assignment. You can inform Deputy Holt that she's free to go."

Thanks for the permission, Finn was tempted to bite out, but he kept his mouth shut. As Parsons strode toward the bull pen, Finn leaned against the wall and

raked his hands through his hair. Lord, he didn't want
to go back in that interrogation room and face Anna.
For the second time in less than a week, he'd questioned
a woman he cared for about a crime she hadn't committed.

Such was the life of a small-town sheriff, he supposed.

But that didn't make it suck any less.

"It wasn't your fault."

Jamie glanced up as Cole entered the bedroom, but
only spared him a brief look before dropping her gaze
to the papers strewn across the bedspread.

Cole stifled a sigh. She'd had her head buried in
those files since one of the FBI agents dropped them off
earlier. They were copies of the documents Sarah had
provided, and Jamie was determined to find something
in those files. Anything that might lead her to Lucy.

"Did you hear me?" Cole said.

She didn't respond.

Releasing the sigh, he sat down at the edge of the
bed, reached over and stilled her hand before she could
pick up the next sheet of paper.

"It's not your fault," he repeated in a firm voice.

She met his eyes, her expression tortured. "I forgot
to set the alarm. I turned my back on Lucy. I let someone knock me out with a crowbar. I lay on the floor unconscious while a baby was stolen." A ragged breath
escaped her mouth. "How is this *not* my fault, Cole?"

"Not everything is in our control, Jamie," he said
quietly. "Crappy things happen sometimes, and we can't
stop them, no matter how hard we try."

His heart ached when he noticed the tears pooling

in the corners of her eyes. "Come here," he murmured, wrapping his arm around her.

She rested her head on his shoulder, trembling slightly. "I just want to find Lucy and bring her back to Sarah."

"You will. *We* will," he corrected. Tucking a strand of auburn hair behind her ears, he leaned in and brushed his lips over hers, then shifted and grabbed the nearest sheet of paper. "Come on, let's go through these together and see if anything jumps out at us."

Jamie smiled through her tears. "You're really going to help?"

"Of course. I want to get Lucy back as much as you do."

He glanced down at the paper, noticing he'd picked up the baby's medical report, which listed Lucy's eye and hair color, blood type, distinguishing birthmarks… Cole's eyes narrowed as something caught his attention.

"Huh," he muttered.

Jamie shot him a sharp look. "Huh what?"

"Did you look at this one?"

He held up the medical report and she furrowed her brow. "Yeah. It's just Lucy's basic information. Why? Do you see something I don't?"

He traced his index finger over one item in particular, watching Jamie's expression as she read the line he'd pointed out. "I don't get it," she said.

Cole didn't answer. His uneasiness grew, slowly coating his stomach until he started to feel sick. He reached up to rub his temples, forcing himself to think logically. This had to be a coincidence.

"Cole, you're scaring me." Her voice became urgent. "Tell me what you're thinking."

Letting out an unsteady breath, he met his fiancée's

worried lavender eyes, opened his mouth, and revealed the frightening suspicion wreaking havoc on his brain.

When he finished, the worry on her face dissolved into apprehension, then sheer resignation. She shook her head a few times, as if trying to comprehend what he'd just told her.

"Well?" he asked. "Do you have anything to say to that?"

She didn't answer for several long moments, and when she finally spoke, she echoed his precise thought on the subject.

"Aw, crap."

Chapter 10

Sarah watched as Finn collected the empty food containers and tossed them in the garbage bin by the back door. They'd stopped to get takeout from the diner after leaving the police station, and had spent the last half hour eating in silence in her spacious kitchen. He hadn't asked to come back to her house, and she hadn't invited, but somehow he'd ended up here and Sarah had to admit, she was grateful for his presence.

The bracelet circling her ankle was a painful reminder that her freedom had been taken away, at least to some extent. She hated that she couldn't get into her car and drive all over the damn state in search of Lucy. She was like a dog chained up in the yard, seeing a squirrel in the distance and being unable to chase after it. She hated feeling so out of control.

She'd felt that way earlier, when she'd practically assaulted Finn in the guest room. At that moment, she'd wanted nothing more than to lose herself in his powerful arms and drugging kisses. The visit to Jason's grave had torn her apart. For that one brief moment, she'd wanted so badly to forget it all. The grief, the worry, the helplessness.

But Finn had been right. It wasn't fair to use him as a means of forgetting.

"Coffee's ready," Finn said.

She glanced up to see him holding two steaming mugs in his hands. "Let's go to the living room," he said with a sigh.

"Do you need to stop by the gallery at some point?" he asked as they left the kitchen. "Anything you need to pick up there?"

The gallery? She'd totally forgotten about it, what with being jailed and then having her daughter taken away from her. She supposed she should put up a sign announcing the place would be closed indefinitely, but the thought of going into town sent dread spiraling through her.

Another thing she'd lost, the gallery she loved. Art had always been her passion. Unfortunately, her hand-eye coordination left much to be desired, and the few times she'd tried drawing or painting had resulted in embarrassment. But she had a good head for business, and she'd majored in it in college, along with a minor in art history. When the gallery had come up for sale, she'd used the money her aunt left her to purchase it, and going to work every morning used to bring her so much joy.

Now she was terrified of facing the citizens of Serenade. Terrified of the whispers and stares she knew she'd encounter.

"I don't need anything," she said softly. "Only my daughter."

She followed him into the living room, and when they were settled on the couch, each on opposite ends, Sarah held her mug between her cold fingers and sighed. "I'm sorry you had to question Anna. I know that must have been hard for you."

He grunted in response, but the pain in his eyes said it all.

"I never thought for a moment she was responsible for any of this," she added. Frustration gathered in her belly. "But who is? Where's Lucy? God, Finn, why was she taken?"

"I don't know," he said in a quiet voice.

Sarah set down her cup on the coffee table and drew up her knees to her chest. She wrapped her arms around herself, wishing it was Lucy she was clinging to instead of her own legs.

"I didn't adopt her to replace him," she whispered.

Finn looked over sharply. "What?"

"Lucy." Her throat burned. "I didn't want her as a replacement for Jason."

"I never thought that was the reason for the adoption."

"No?"

"No," he said firmly. His features creased. "But four years ago, when you…"

Shame tugged at her. "When I pressured you to try for another baby? I shouldn't have done that. It wasn't fair to you. Wasn't fair to either one of us." A heavy sigh escaped her mouth. "You were right, you know. That time, I *was* trying to find a replacement. I just wanted Jason back so badly. Having another child was the only way I thought of to make it happen, but I re-

alize now that it was a mistake. Jason couldn't be re-
placed."

"No," he said thickly. "He couldn't."

"I'm sorry, Finn."

"So am I."

They fell quiet, each lost in their own thoughts, until
the doorbell rang and squashed the first sense of peace
she'd felt in days.

"I'll get it," Finn said, standing up.

He left the room, returning a few moments later with
Jamie and Cole in tow. Sarah instantly tensed when she
caught the identical expressions on the couple's faces.
Something was up, she could sense it.

"I hope we weren't interrupting," Jamie said, fidgeting with her hands.

Sarah studied the other woman's face. Something
was up, all right. "No, it's fine. What's going on?"

"Cole and I had something we needed to discuss
with you."

"Sit down," Finn offered, gesturing to the two arm-
chairs opposite the couch. "I'll get you guys some
coffee."

"No," they said in unison.

Sarah's eyebrows rose.

"I just want to get this over with," Cole added, his
face awash with reluctance. "Let's not waste time."

As Cole and Jamie sat down, Finn joined Sarah on
the couch. This time, he sat right beside her, and her
heart did a little lurch as he took her hand in his. She
could tell he felt the same unease, picked up on the
black cloud that seemed to creep into the room and
hang over their heads like a canopy.

"What the hell is going on?" Finn burst out when

neither Cole nor Jamie said a word. "You're scaring Sarah. Hell, you're scaring me a little, too."

Jamie cleared her throat. "Okay. Well. Cole and I were going over the files Sarah gave Parsons and his team. We may have found something."

Sarah squeezed Finn's hand, unable to stop the hope that soared along her spine. "Something that might lead us to Lucy?"

Jamie and Cole exchanged troubled looks. "Maybe," Jamie said. "But first... Cole, you say it. I still don't even know if I believe it."

Cole leaned forward in his chair, clasping his hands on his lap. "Like Jamie said, we were looking at the files, and I noticed something in one of Lucy's medical records. She has a birthmark on her left shoulder, shaped like a—"

"Star," Sarah finished. She shot him a confused look. "I don't get it. Why is that important?"

"It may not be. Except..."

"Except what?" Finn barked. "Where are you going with this, Donovan?"

"Teresa had a star-shaped birthmark on her left shoulder," Cole blurted out.

Sarah gaped at him in shock. Well, she hadn't been expecting that. But what on earth was he getting at? So what if Cole's ex-wife had a similar birthmark as Lucy?

She quickly voiced her thoughts. "Lots of people have birthmarks. It's just a coincidence."

"Are you sure about that?" Jamie asked in a soft voice.

Sarah bristled. "What are you saying? That because Teresa and Lucy have star-shaped marks on their shoulders, then they're...what, related?"

Nobody said a word.

The implication settled over Sarah like a patch of thick fog. No. No, that was absolutely *ridiculous*. Strictly coincidence. Teresa had a birthmark. Lucy had a birthmark. Big deal. That didn't mean Teresa was...

"She's not Lucy's mother!" Sarah exploded, stunned that anyone could even think it. "Birthmarks aren't even hereditary. This is just a weird coincidence."

"Sarah," Cole began. He stopped, cleared his throat, and plowed on. "It's not just the birthmark. That's what caught my attention, because Teresa's mark was so damn distinct, you know? But Jamie and I were talking it over, and we realized there might be more."

"Teresa left town nine months ago," Jamie spoke up. "She told everyone she was moving to Raleigh to start a new life and put this sorry town behind her. She was gone for six months and came back to Serenade three months ago—the same time you brought Lucy home."

"That doesn't mean anything. She wasn't pregnant when she left," Sarah protested. "People would have noticed."

"She only would've been three months along. Early enough that she wouldn't be showing," Jamie said.

Sarah's mind was reeling. This was absurd. Teresa lived in Raleigh for six months. Sarah had adopted Lucy from Raleigh. This wasn't one of those dumb riddles—Bob is a lawyer, lawyers are sharks, therefore Bob is a shark. There was no proof, nothing written in bright neon announcing that Teresa Donovan had given birth to Lucy.

She suddenly grew light-headed. Letting go of Finn's hand, she rubbed her forehead, trying to clear her brain. Lucy was hers. *Hers.* She'd sat in a hotel room for two days while the birth mother was in labor. She'd held her for the first time in the nursery at Raleigh General.

She'd brought her home to Serenade—one week after Teresa changed her mind about the mysterious relocation to Raleigh.

No.

Coincidence.

Black dots moved in front of her eyes, making her sag forward.

"She's *not* Lucy's mother," she choked out. "She can't be…"

God, what if it was true?

What if Teresa Donovan had left town to conceal her pregnancy, given birth to Lucy and put her up for adoption?

What if Sarah had adopted *Teresa's* baby?

The breath drained from her lungs, while her palms went damp and started to tingle.

She heard Finn's voice saying her name, but it sounded distant, muffled. The black dots got bigger, shrouding her vision. She leaned forward, trying to breathe through a fresh wave of dizziness.

And then she fainted.

"Damn it, Jamie," Finn snapped as he held Sarah's unconscious body in his arms. "Why the hell did you two have to come here and drop this on her? It might not even be true!"

Jamie probably answered, but he didn't hear a damn word. Sarah had fallen off the couch when she'd passed out, her right temple snapping against the leg of the coffee table. She wasn't waking up, and panic rapidly entered his bloodstream, making it hard to think clearly.

"Call Bennett," he ordered as he cradled Sarah's head in his lap.

He pushed dark strands from her face, gently stroking her cheek as he said, "Wake up, sweetheart. Come on, Sarah, wake up."

He heard Cole talking on his cell phone, but all he could focus on was Sarah. Her face was completely devoid of color, save for the slight redness at her temple. She hadn't hit her head too badly, or at least it didn't look like it, but it worried him that she was still out cold.

Fighting a rush of anxiety, he pinched one of her cheeks, then cupped her chin. "Sarah...baby...open your eyes."

There was a soft moan, and she stirred in his arms, bringing an explosion of sweet relief to his body. He watched as her eyelids fluttered and then opened. Mystification swarmed her gaze as she stared up at him.

"Finn?" she mumbled.

"It's me. I'm here," he said roughly.

She shifted, slowly twisting her head. "I...passed out?"

"Yeah, you were out for a few minutes." He helped her into a sitting position, wrapping an arm around her as they sat there on the hardwood floor. Jamie and Cole were standing, each one donning a look of remorse.

Good, let them feel bad. What had they been thinking, showing up here and revealing that Teresa Donovan, the wicked witch of Serenade, could possibly be the biological mother of Sarah's adopted daughter?

His teeth clenched at the mere thought of it. Sure, he'd always thought it strange that Teresa had left town for no apparent reason, only to waltz back six months later as if she hadn't even been gone. But that was Teresa for you. Unpredictable, impulsive.

Manipulative, evil...

Hell, he didn't blame Sarah for fainting from the news.

"Bennett's on his way," Cole announced.

"Travis?" Sarah cried, her head snapping up. "No, call him and tell him not to come. I'm fine."

"You hit your head," Finn replied tersely. "I want to make sure you don't have a concussion."

She blew out a frustrated breath, wiggling from his embrace. "I don't have a concussion. I just fainted."

She tried standing, but he noticed her legs were still shaky and promptly rose to help steady her. And then it was him and Sarah, facing off with Cole and Jamie. Tension filled the air.

"It can't be true," Sarah finally said. "I know you guys think it might be, but I refuse to believe that Teresa gave birth to my daughter."

"Then you won't mind if I get my P.I. to investigate," Cole said gruffly.

From the corner of his eye, Finn saw Sarah blanch. "What?" she protested. "No."

"I know you don't want to believe it, but we need to find out if it's true," Jamie said in a gentle tone. "Sarah, if Teresa is Lucy's biological mother, then that changes everything."

"How?" Sarah whispered. "How does it change anything? Lucy is still mine. She's *my* daughter, Jamie!"

"Of course she is, honey. I just meant that it could shed new light on the abduction."

Finn's shoulders straightened. Damn. As much as he hated to even consider the possibility, the birthmark and Teresa's abrupt disappearance were hard to ignore. Jamie was right. If the unthinkable really was true, then Lucy's kidnapping could be connected to that. The Bureau had been looking into people who might hold a grudge against Sarah, people who might want to punish her by stealing her child, but if the child was *Teresa's…*

well, that could provide a different motive. A different suspect.

"The biological father," Jamie spoke up, as if reading Finn's thoughts. "That's just one example of someone who might've taken Lucy."

Finn stiffened as a nauseating thought occurred to him. "I swear to God, Donovan, if you're the father of that baby..."

Cole flinched as if he'd been struck by a fist. "What? *No.* Teresa and I had already been separated when she moved to Raleigh."

"And you didn't get together at all?" Finn asked with narrowed eyes.

"I would rather have waxed my back than touch that woman." With the contempt dripping from his tone, Cole's declaration was more than convincing.

Jamie held up her hand. "We're getting off track here. Cole is not the father. We don't even know if Teresa is the *mother.* But Sarah, we need to pursue this. We need to."

Sarah sagged against him and Finn felt her resolve begin to crumble. "Fine," she relented, glancing at Cole. "Get your investigator to look into it, but don't feel bad about wasting your money if this leads to a dead end." She stuck out her chin. "Which I think it will be."

Cole was already flipping open his cell phone and moving toward the doorway. Jamie shot Sarah an apologetic look. "I guess we'll head home, then. I'm so sorry for giving you such a shock. But Cole and I spoke about it and decided we had no choice but to tell you about our suspicions. We weren't trying to hurt you, Sarah, please believe that."

Sarah let out a sigh. "I'm sorry I freaked. I know

you weren't trying to hurt me. Like you said, it was a shock."

Although he was reluctant to let go of her arm, Finn did, so he could escort Cole and Jamie to the door. He couldn't resist frowning at the two of them as they left Sarah's house.

When he walked back to the living room, he forced Sarah to lie down, despite her insistence that she was perfectly all right. He asked her to humor him, which she did, though her lips twitched when he shoved a pillow behind her head.

He wasn't sure why he was acting like a mother hen, but he couldn't shove away the image of Sarah collapsing onto the floor, or her pale, unconscious face. At least the doctor would be here soon, though Finn tensed when he realized he'd pretty much just given Travis Bennett an invitation to come over and spend time with Sarah.

They were just friends, she'd told him the other day. He clung to those four words, determined to keep his growing jealousy at bay, but when Bennett showed up ten minutes later, Finn had trouble controlling himself.

"Sarah, are you all right?" Travis demanded when he saw her sprawled on the couch.

Friends, his ass. The way Bennett charged toward her like a damn white knight was hard to ignore. So was the way the good doctor knelt by the sofa and proceeded to put his hands all over her.

All right, one hand. And he was just examining the red spot on Sarah's temple. Nevertheless, the sight of another man touching Sarah made Finn see stars. Breathing through the sudden onslaught of protectiveness, he stood at the opposite end of the couch, keeping his hands pressed tightly to his sides.

When Bennett finally took his hand back, Finn let out a slow breath. "It's not a concussion," Bennett concluded, smiling down at Sarah. "Your pupils are fine, no nausea and you're completely coherent. I think you'll live."

Finn gritted his teeth when Sarah returned the doctor's smile. And then his jaw almost cracked when she reached to touch Bennett's arm. "Thanks, Travis. I wasn't worried, but Finn is a little overprotective."

Bennett glanced at Finn with warm brown eyes. "Well, not to worry, Sheriff. She'll be just fine."

"Then I guess you can be leaving now, doc," Finn said brusquely. "I'll take it from here."

With a tender smile, Bennett reached out to give Sarah's arm a squeeze.

Finn clenched his jaw again.

"Take it easy tonight," Bennett told his patient. "And remember, don't hesitate to call if you need anything."

"I'll take care of her," Finn practically snapped, advancing on the doctor.

Taking the hint, Bennett zipped up his black Windbreaker and allowed Finn to march him out the door. When Finn returned to the living room, Sarah was sitting up, a frown marring her mouth.

"You didn't have to be so rude to him," she said coldly.

"I didn't like the way he was touching you," he retorted, a note of anger in his voice.

"He was examining me. At *your* request." She blew a stray strand of hair out of her face, her frown deepening. "What's your problem with him, anyway? Travis is a nice man."

Finn mumbled something under his breath.

"Was that even English?" she demanded. "Seriously,

Finn, quit acting like a damn caveman. Travis is my friend, and I didn't appreciate the way you treated him."

"And I didn't appreciate him *touching* you," he grumbled back.

She shook her head, her liquid brown eyes filling with amazement. "So what if he touched me? Why do you care if—"

"Because *I* want to be the one touching you," he interrupted, frustration coursing through his blood. "Because I want to be your damn *friend.*" He cursed loudly. "No, scratch that, I don't want to be your friend, Sarah. I want to be your *everything.*"

She went stricken. "What…what are you saying exactly?"

"I'm saying I love you."

The baby wouldn't stop crying. She'd endured three hours of Lucy's earsplitting howls and it was beginning to seriously try her patience. She wasn't sure she blamed the baby, though. She was pretty miserable, too, holed up in this isolated cabin instead of boarding a plane that would take them to the Bahamas. But arrangements were still being made for the little beach house in Nassau, and there was no way she could show up at the airport with Lucy in her arms. No, not until the media storm died down and news of the kidnapping faded from people's minds.

She rocked Lucy in her arms, watching the rain streak the dirty windowpane. The baby's sobs were finally ebbing, much to her relief.

"I know you don't like it here," she murmured. "I don't, either. But I promise you, it's only temporary. Soon we'll be somewhere warm and sunny, and we'll walk along the sand and look at the ocean…."

Lucy's tiny eyelids started fluttering.

She experienced a burst of joy. Was the baby starting to feel comfortable with her? It was about time. She was Lucy's mother now, and these past two days of hearing Lucy cry and cry hadn't been a walk in the park.

As the baby slept in her arms, she gazed dreamily out the window, pretending she was looking at the calm turquoise ocean in the Bahamas. Soon. God, soon.

The cell phone on the little wooden table beside the rocking chair started to vibrate, yanking her from her happy thoughts. Shifting the baby, she snatched up the phone and pressed Talk before the vibrations woke Lucy.

"It's about time," she said after recognizing the caller ID. "You said you'd call four hours ago."

"I know. I'm sorry." The voice on the other end of the line sounded strained. "I had some things to take care of."

"I hope you're referring to the travel arrangements," she snapped, "because I'm getting sick of this place. So is Lucy."

"I'm doing everything I can, but we discussed this. The kidnapping is all over the news. Lucy needs to stay hidden for a while."

She frowned. "How long is a while?"

"Until people forget about her. Until you can take her out in public without someone yelling *kidnapper* and calling the police."

Valid point. She bit back the urge to argue, knowing that hiding was the smartest move at the moment.

"But you're making plans," she pressed, unable to mask the urgency in her tone.

"Of course I am." There was a pause. "Don't worry,

everything is under control. Just stay inside and take care of the baby. I'll call you tomorrow."

She hung up the phone and cuddled the baby against her breasts, happiness suffusing her body and bringing a rush of serenity.

"Soon," she whispered to the sleeping child. "We'll get out of here soon, baby girl. And then we'll disappear, far away, where nobody can ever take you away from me."

Chapter 11

Sarah was dizzy again, only this time it had nothing to do with her recent fainting spell and everything to do with the fact that Finn had just said he'd loved her.

A part of her was basking in the warmth of those three words, fighting the temptation to hurl herself into his arms and never let go. But that was the old Sarah. The one who'd been madly in love with this man and dreamed of sharing her life with him.

The new Sarah was older. Wiser. The new Sarah had put the past behind her and accepted that she and Patrick Finnegan were simply not meant to be. They'd had their shot over four years ago. And they'd failed. When a cruel twist of fate had mercilessly destroyed their lives, they'd had a choice: swim together or sink alone.

Well, Sarah had wound up at the bottom of a cold, dark abyss. She'd drowned in grief and depression, wildly flailing her arms in hopes that Finn would pull her out of that terrible place. But he hadn't been there for her.

So go ahead and call her a coward, but she had no intention of drowning again, and that's what getting involved with Finn represented to her.

"Did you hear me?" he asked gruffly, slowly sinking down on the other end of the sofa.

"I heard you," she murmured.

His blue eyes narrowed. "And you have nothing to say? No reaction?"

Sighing, she linked her fingers together and rested them on her thighs. "What is there to say? I'm sure you meant what you said, but—"

"Damn right, I meant it. I love you, Sarah. I've loved you since the day we ran into each other at the lake."

She fought the wave of nostalgia that swelled in her belly. "That was a long time ago."

"Maybe it was. But my feelings for you have never changed."

He edged closer, so that his hard thigh was inches from her socked feet. She wanted to pull her legs up, to avoid contact, but she was rooted in place, drawn to the fierce look on his handsome face.

"I'm a different man, sweetheart," he began, his voice raspy and thick with emotion. "Back then, I wasn't strong enough to handle everything that happened. I left because I didn't have the balls to fix things, and it's a choice I've regretted every day for these last few years."

Exasperation rose in her throat. "We can't keep talking about this, over and over again. You already told me all of this, and I believe you, Finn. I truly believe you regret what happened between us." She drew much-needed air into her lungs. "And I can see that you've changed. You're more mature, calmer. I see that."

He sounded as frustrated as she felt. "Then why are you holding back? Why not give us another chance?"

"Because I've changed, too."

Finn looked startled by her admission. "What do you mean?"

"I mean that I'm not the same twenty-three year old who buried her son. I had a mental breakdown, for God's sake. I spent two years in therapy trying to put my life back together piece by piece. I grew up, too."

"Then we're both in a better place. A healthier place." He let out a breath. "Let me prove to you that I can be different this time around. That I can be there for you, and take care of you."

"Take care of me? You arrested me!" A muscle in her jaw twitched. "Besides, I can take care of myself."

"I know you can. That's not what I meant." He looked frazzled. "I'm just saying I want another chance."

"And I'm saying I don't think I want to give it to you."

Pain descended on his face, but since she'd already come this far, she might as well finish.

"I don't trust you, Finn. And I don't have that same rosy outlook you suddenly seem to possess. Obstacles are always going to pop up. Even if we did get back together, there would be rough patches, arguments." She swallowed. "I don't trust that you'll stick around."

"You'll never know if you don't give me a chance."

"Maybe if I didn't have Lucy, I could do that. But I'm a mother now. I need to provide stability for my child, to give her a happy, healthy life. What if I bring you into our home and she gets attached to you, only to be abandoned if things get too tough for you again? I won't take that chance."

He recoiled as if she'd slapped him. And then his features went hard. "I won't give up, you know. I will make you trust me again, Sarah."

She almost smiled. The steely resolve in his eyes was so achingly familiar. She was reminded of that bad boy who'd been determined to win her over all those years ago. On their first date, he'd pushed for a second. On their second, a third. When she'd gotten cold feet about moving in with him, he'd seduced her with red roses and a gourmet dinner and mind-blowing sex, until she'd given in.

Not that it had been a chore. Back then she would've done anything to be with this man. Nobody knew her like Finn. They *got* each other. They both tended to be too serious, neither was quick to laugh, but together, they laughed and teased and spoke of things neither of them had told anyone else before. She'd always been scared of that deep bond, that unbreakable connection.

Well, not so unbreakable. Finn had severed it when he'd walked out the door.

And she hadn't been lying. Maybe things could have been different if Lucy weren't in her life. Maybe she could have risked her heart and allowed him back in. But she would never risk her daughter's heart. Never.

Finn's cell phone jolted her back to reality. Saved by the foghorn. She got the feeling they would've talked around in circles if not for the interruption, and though the twinge of hurt in Finn's eyes made her heart ache, she was glad she'd told him where she stood.

Finn glanced at the screen, then muttered an explative.

Sarah's heart stopped. "Is it about Lucy?"

"No, it's the D.A." He lifted the phone to his ear and said, "Finnegan."

Sarah watched with growing anxiety as Finn spoke with Jonas Gregory. Well, Finn did most of the listening, and whatever Gregory was saying, Finn didn't look happy. He said "Yes, sir" several times, and at one point, she noticed his fingers tightening over the phone, knuckles turning white.

When he finally hung up, her anxiety was at an all-time high. "What did he say? Was it about the case?"

Finn gave a quick nod.

"What did he say?" she repeated.

After a second of visible reluctance, Finn spoke. "He wants me to send him a report and some supporting documents of the evidence against you. He's taking the case to the grand jury for an indictment."

The breath drained from her lungs. "What does that mean?"

"The grand jury will decide the charges that will officially be brought against you."

She swallowed. "But they might also dismiss the case altogether, right?"

"It's possible but unlikely. I think you're going to be indicted, Sarah."

She suddenly felt really, really cold. "When is Gregory meeting with them?"

"Monday."

Monday. That gave them five days. Five days to find Lucy and catch Teresa's real killer. Talk about pressure.

Fortunately, Finn looked shockingly calm about it. She watched as determination crept into his blue eyes, burning like a roaring bonfire. "When I told you I would get you out of this mess, I meant it," he said sternly. "I won't let you go to prison for something you didn't do."

"And if I'm indicted? If I'm *convicted*?" She couldn't keep the terror from her voice.

His jaw hardened. "You won't go to jail. Even if I have to whisk you from the damn country, you won't be going to jail."

Shock crashed into her like a tidal wave. Was she hearing him right? Had he actually just admitted he'd break the law before letting her be incarcerated?

For one long moment, she was tempted to take back everything she'd said only minutes ago. Maybe she *could* trust him again. Maybe that leap of faith he'd begged her to take didn't have such a steep drop. Finn loved his job. He was proud of his position, his service to the people of Serenade. If he could even consider throwing it away just to help her, then maybe he truly *had* changed. Enough to merit a second chance.

Her mind started spinning again. It seemed to be doing that a lot these days.

God, she couldn't think about this anymore. Not when her daughter was missing. Lucy was her main focus right now—her *only* focus.

And everything else, her conflicting feelings for Patrick Finnegan, her fear and doubts, heck, even her impending indictment…it would all take the backseat until her daughter was returned to her arms, safe and sound.

Sarah walked into the living room the next morning and found Finn sprawled on her sofa, dead to the world. Her breath caught in her throat at the sight of him. He wore nothing but a pair of black boxer-briefs that couldn't hide the impressive bulge at his groin. She swept her gaze over his bare chest and admired his defined pectorals, the dusting of dark hair that led to his waistband. Her heart thumped in a persistent drumbeat, getting faster as she stared at his muscular thighs, the long legs dangling off the end of her couch. He was the most perfect male specimen, all muscle and sinew and sleek golden skin.

She couldn't help but smile at the way he had one arm flung haphazardly over the side of the sofa. He'd always had the habit of stretching out in his sleep. She couldn't count how many times she'd woken up curled into a tiny ball at the very edge of the bed while Finn monopolized all the space.

Deciding not to wake him, she went into the kitchen to brew a pot of coffee, her smile fading when she noticed Lucy's bouncy seat on the table. Pain somersaulted inside her chest. God, why hadn't they found Lucy yet? Finn had assured her that Parsons and the other agents were doing everything they could. Apparently the Bureau's kidnapping unit had alerted all the major airports and border crossings, providing photos of Lucy and ordering officials to keep their eyes out for anyone traveling with a child matching Lucy's description. But other than the tip from the boutique owner in Grayden, none of the leads that had come in had amounted to anything.

Sarah poured herself some coffee, but the hot liquid didn't erase the chill in her body. She wanted her baby back, damn it. Her gaze dropped to her ankle monitor and she experienced a burst of anger. She couldn't even search for Lucy outside Serenade. She'd never felt so powerless before, not since she'd lost Jason.

Footsteps came from the hallway and then Finn appeared, rubbing the sleep from his eyes. He'd put on his jeans and the gray sweatshirt he'd had on yesterday. "Morning," he murmured. "Will you pour me a cup while I go wash up?"

"Sure."

He left the kitchen and she stood there, staring at the empty doorway. She wasn't sure why he'd even stayed the night, especially after the exasperating heart-to-heart they'd shared, but Finn had insisted he didn't want her to be alone. She didn't like admitting it, not even to herself, but she'd felt comforted when she slid into bed last night, knowing he was right downstairs.

Not that she'd slept. She'd tossed and turned the entire night, thinking of Lucy and Finn and Jason and everything she'd lost.

"Jamie and Cole are on their way over," Finn announced when he strode back into the room ten minutes later. He accepted the mug she handed him and took a long sip.

Sarah's heart dropped. "Why? Did Cole's P.I. find something?"

"Jamie didn't say. She only said they were coming."

Putting down her cup, she ignored the uneasy feeling in the pit of her stomach and headed for the door. "I guess I'll shower and dress, then."

She quickly hurried upstairs and showered, then slipped into a pair of black yoga pants and a stretchy green V-neck sweater, not bothering with a bra. Panic rose inside her as she dressed. Her hands wouldn't quit shaking, making it tough to roll on her black ankle socks. Why were Cole and Jamie coming over? What had they found out?

She'd been trying desperately not to think about what they'd told her yesterday, but now the frightening prospect returned in full force, causing her hand to tremble even harder as she ran a brush through her damp hair.

What if Teresa was Lucy's biological mother?

The brush dropped from her hand and fell onto the vanity table as she contemplated the outrageous thought. She'd despised Teresa Donovan. Teresa had been the cruelest woman Sarah had ever met. She slept around, went after other women's husbands, mocked people for the fun of it. Sarah had always believed that every human being possessed one redeemable quality, had *something* good about them, but not Teresa. That woman hadn't been human.

She'd been a monster.

Sarah stared at her reflection in the mirror, finally finding the courage to ask the one question she'd been avoiding since Cole and Jamie had shared their suspicions.

Would she love Lucy less if Teresa turned out to be the baby's birth mother?

The second the thought entered her brain, fury rose up her chest and clamped around her throat. No. *No.* She would love Lucy just the same, and *that* revelation grabbed the anger and transformed it into soaring liberation.

Lucy was *her* daughter. It didn't matter who gave birth to her. She was *hers.*

Squaring her shoulders, Sarah went back downstairs, picking up on the murmur of voices coming from the kitchen. Cole and Jamie were here. So was Agent Parsons, she discovered in dismay when she walked into the room. The fair-haired man was helping himself to a cup of coffee, and he greeted her with a smirk when she entered.

"Good morning, Ms. Connelly."

"Morning," she muttered before turning to the couple sitting at the table. "What did you find out?"

"I'm wondering the same thing," Parsons said. He frowned at Finn. "I see you've been running some sort of side investigation, and I don't appreciate being kept out of the loop."

"Oh, relax, Mark," Jamie grumbled with a frown of her own. "Finn had nothing to do with this. Cole and I ran this lead all by ourselves."

"And why is that?" Parsons asked, his nasty stare now directed at the auburn-haired profiler. "As I recall, you took a leave of absence. You have no business interfering with this case."

Sarah tried not to raise her eyebrows. The animosity between Jamie and Parsons was palpable. She hadn't noticed it before, when they'd both been here the morning after Lucy was taken. But now it was obvious there was no love lost between the two of them, and Jamie's hostile reaction to the man only reaffirmed Sarah's own dislike. Jamie was the most levelheaded person she'd ever met; if she didn't like Parsons, then that meant he truly was the pompous jerk Sarah had pegged him to be.

Jamie scowled. "Mark, why don't you just drink your coffee and let Cole tell everyone what we found out, okay?"

Parsons looked like he was inwardly seething, but he kept his mouth shut, gesturing for Cole to take over.

"My private investigator visited the adoption clinic yesterday evening, but as expected, they refused to divulge any records without a warrant." Cole spared a glance at the federal agent. "Perhaps you can arrange for one, if you see fit. Anyway, after my guy struck out, he visited several hospitals in the area and did some digging."

Sarah bit the inside of her cheek. "And?"

"And he found a record indicating that Teresa was admitted into St. Mary's Hospital on June 23." Cole paused in discomfort. "She gave birth to a baby girl."

Sarah gasped, leaning against the counter for support. June 23. That was the birth date the adoption clinic had provided her for Lucy. Oh, God. It was actually *true*.

"There was a birth certificate on record, listing Teresa as the mother, though she used her maiden name. The father was unknown. After that, my guy worked backward, tracking down the clinic Teresa visited during her pregnancy. She had monthly checkups and apparently took good care of herself. She put her own name on the birth certificate, but everything else she did while using the name Valerie Matthews."

"Are we sure it's Teresa then?" Finn said in a clipped tone. "Maybe Valerie is the one who gave birth."

Cole shook his head. "It's not possible. Valerie was here in town when Teresa moved to Raleigh. I ran into her several times." He scowled. "She loved to yell at me about divorcing her sister."

Finn let out a breath. "Yeah, you're right. I remember seeing her around, too, and she definitely wasn't pregnant."

"Ahem."

Everyone turned toward Parsons, who was angrily setting down his mug, his eyes flashing with irritation. "Are you saying that Teresa Donovan was the biological mother of Ms. Connelly's child?"

Jamie shot him a *duh* look. "Yes, Mark, that's what we're saying."

He went silent for a moment, then twisted around in his chair. Sarah found a pair of ice-blue eyes staring her down.

"Is that why you killed her?" he asked pleasantly.

The air swooshed from her lungs. *"What?"*

Finn was already scraping back his chair. "What the *hell*—"

Parsons stood before Finn could even finish the outraged exclamation. Crossing his arms over his chest, the agent glanced at Jamie with a cold smile. "You realize you've only succeeded in strengthening my case, right, Crawford?"

Her lavender eyes blazed. "What are you talking about?"

"Motive, Crawford." Parsons turned to bestow that same reptilian smile on Sarah. "You found out Mrs. Donovan was your child's mother, didn't you, Sarah? Was she regretting the adoption? Did she want her baby back?"

Sarah felt as if someone had slapped her. "What? No!"

"Did you kill her when she threatened to fight for her child? With your mental illness, you probably just snapped, didn't you, Sarah? She wanted her kid back, and you shot her in the—"

"Enough!"

Finn's roar reverberated in the kitchen. Before Sarah could blink, he had Parsons by the collar and was slamming the other man against her bright yellow wall. The anger rolling off Finn's big body spiked the temperature in the room by a hundred degrees, and she suddenly couldn't tear her eyes off him. Here he was, the sexy macho jerk she'd fallen for all those years ago, with that possessiveness that made her want to clobber him and at the same time melted her heart.

"Watch your mouth, you son of a bitch!" He shook Parsons hard, and Sarah's eyes widened. "She didn't kill anybody."

Parsons's face was beet red, his breaths coming in harsh pants. With his palms pushed against Finn's chest, he sidestepped his hold, his eyes wild as he glared at the man who'd just accosted him. "I'll have your damn badge for this, Finnegan! How dare you lay a hand on me!"

Finn was breathing just as hard. "You were out of line, Parsons."

"Why, because you're sleeping with her?" the other man spat out. "That's another reason I'll fight to get your badge taken away."

Finn looked ready to launch himself at the agent again, and this time Sarah refused to let him do it. It might have brought a tiny spark of pleasure, watching him defend her like that, but she wasn't going to let him throw away the career he'd worked hard to obtain because of some slimy jerk.

"Stop it," she ordered, her sharp tone snapping in the air like a whip. "I won't have you brawling in my kitchen like a bunch of damn teenagers. My daughter is *missing!*"

Both men went shamefaced, though she noticed neither one apologized. To each other, anyway. But Finn did shoot her a sheepish look and murmur, "I'm sorry." He slowly unclenched his fists. "You're right. Lucy is all that matters. The only thing we should be doing right now is finding her."

"And I think I have an idea about who may have taken her," Jamie spoke up from across the room.

Sarah spun around. "Who?" she demanded.

"Yes, Crawford," came Parsons's mocking voice. "Who took the child?"

Jamie got to her feet and approached the tense group. "You said so yourself, Mark. In child abductions, a family member is usually the perpetrator."

The agent's eyes narrowed. "Are you suggesting the child's biological father is responsible?"

"He could be, but that's not who I had in mind." Jamie gave a wry shrug. "Seeing as Teresa had more lovers than Hugh Hefner, I doubt she even knew who the father was, and if she did, I can't see her informing him that he was going to be a daddy." She slanted her head. "No, I'm thinking a different kind of family member."

Sarah gasped, the thought slicing into her brain just as Jamie voiced it.

"I think Valerie Matthews did it. Lucy's aunt."

Chapter 12

"No answer," Finn said grimly, striding up to the Jeep where Anna waited.

They were parked in front of Valerie Matthews's small townhouse, located in a residential area a few blocks from Main Street. Valerie hadn't come to the door when he'd rang the doorbell, and from the days' worth of mail piled up on her front stoop, it was clear she hadn't been home in a while. According to the law office she worked at, Valerie had taken a leave of absence one week ago. Personal time, she'd told the senior partner at the firm, claiming she planned on traveling for a couple months. But Finn didn't buy it. Not one bit.

Valerie had taken Lucy. They might not have proof of it, and hell, no evidence that Valerie had even been aware of her sister's pregnancy, but Finn's instincts rarely failed him and they were pointing all sorts of fingers at Valerie Matthews.

"She's not there, huh?" Anna said quietly.

"No, I think she's already skipped town."

"With Lucy?"

He gave a harsh nod. "I'd bet my life on it."

They both grew silent, frustration building in the air. And tension. He was suddenly aware of that, too, and guilt prickled his skin as he met his deputy's eyes.

"Anna," he started roughly, "I wanted to—"

"Apologize?" she filled in, her dark eyes twinkling.

Her playful expression caught him off guard. "I can't even begin to tell you how sorry I am that I had to question you," he said. "I never thought for a minute you had anything to do with Lucy's kidnapping."

The young woman sighed. "You were covering all your bases. I know that, boss. Can't say it didn't sting a little, though."

His guilt deepened, filling his belly. Lord, he was just alienating everyone around him, wasn't he? Arresting Sarah, interrogating Anna.

"You've definitely had a streak of bad luck," Anna said, as if reading his mind. "First Cole, then Sarah, now me."

He swallowed down a gulp of anguish, but she hurried on before he could apologize again. "Nobody thinks it's your fault, boss. A woman was murdered. A baby was abducted. I know you have a job to do, no matter where the evidence takes you."

Her gentle reassurance brought a rush of peace. He'd needed to hear that. He'd worked damn hard to get to where he was, going from a punk with a chip on his shoulder to a devoted deputy under the former sheriff. When he'd been elected to serve his townspeople, he'd never felt prouder. For years, he'd been sullen, miserable, lashing out at anyone in his path because the one person he really wanted to strike out at—his mother—was too fragile and messed up, already a victim of something completely out of her control.

But he'd battled the anger and bitterness and turned things around for himself. Being Serenade's sheriff gave him a sense of worth, a sense of belonging. Yet it didn't give him the sense of sheer *completeness* that Sarah did.

He loved his job, but Sarah...that was a whole different kind of love. She brightened his life in a way nobody ever could. She was so damn smart, so kind and patient. She could light up a room with her smile, and when she was happy, that happiness soared outward and made him feel as though he'd been touched by a ray of sunshine.

He was determined to win her back. Now that he knew the reasons holding her back, her fear that he'd abandon her and her daughter, he was determined to prove her wrong.

"So, what now?" Anna asked, interrupting the detour of his thoughts. "How do we track down Valerie?"

Finn's phone came to life then, and he quickly pulled it out of his pocket. He glanced at the caller ID and nodded in satisfaction. "Hopefully this will point us in the right direction."

"Finn, my investigator just left the adoption clinic in Raleigh," Cole barked in his ear, getting right to the point.

"And?"

"Valerie knew about Lucy."

The confirmation sent a streak of triumph through him. "You sure?"

"Oh, yeah." Cole made an unintelligible sound. "I swear, those Matthews women know how to get what

they want. My P.I. flashed her picture to the employ-
ees—this time the director let him inside the clinic.
Apparently she realized a missing child was more important than red tape. She claims that she never released
Lucy's file to anyone, but my guy got a suspicious feeling about one of the lab techs working there.

"He talked to the kid alone, got him to admit that
he'd let Valerie into the records room about a month
after Teresa was killed." Cole swore in annoyance. "She
seduced the poor guy, right in the damn file room. He
left her alone for ten minutes, and when he came back,
she was gone. He couldn't be sure she got a look at any
of the files, but I'm inclined to think she did."

"Me, too," Finn said with a sigh. He mulled it over.
"So somehow she figured Teresa had been pregnant,
and she got her confirmation by checking the adoption
files. She found out Sarah was the adoptive mother, and
took it upon herself to steal the baby."

"Or she had help," Cole offered. "Jamie wasn't sure
if the attacker was a man or a woman. Valerie could
have arranged for someone to take Lucy."

"Maybe, but at the moment, Valerie's the only one
we're certain about." Finn's lips tightened. "She has the
baby, Cole. What's your investigator doing to track her
down?"

"He's going over her credit card records as we speak,
but we're not hopeful about it. She wouldn't be stupid
enough to leave a paper trail."

"You never know. Another thing about the Matthews
women—they act first, think later. We just need to pray
that she slipped up."

"I'll keep you posted."

Finn hung up and tucked the phone away, turning to
Anna with a hard look. "Valerie knew about Lucy."

"I got that much from your side of the conversation." She was already moving to the passenger side of the Jeep. "What do we do now?"

He slid into the driver's seat and started the engine. "I'll drop you off at the station, and then I'm heading to Sarah's. I'll call you once I hear from Cole. If we find out where Valerie's hiding, I want you and Max with me."

Anna's brown eyes shone with pleasure. "Really?"

He took his hand off the gearshift and lightly touched her arm. "I already told you once, but I'll say it again. Neither Sarah nor I thought you took that child. You're a terrific cop, Anna, and I feel better knowing you have my back."

She murmured a soft thank-you, and Finn could feel the tension leaving her body. At least one woman in his life was capable of forgiving him.

Now he just needed to win over Sarah.

"What do you mean, I have to stay here?" Sarah demanded after he'd told her where he was going.

Finn smothered a sigh as he noticed her outraged expression and the determined slash of her mouth. Damn it, he knew that stubborn look. It probably mirrored his own.

They'd received the news from Cole's investigator ten minutes after Finn strode into Sarah's house. Valerie Matthews had purchased groceries eighteen hours ago at a gas station in Holliday, a small county two towns over from Serenade. The purchase might not mean anything—could've been a pit stop on her way out of state, making her long gone by now—but they couldn't very well ignore it, either.

Holliday was a tiny township, consisting of a handful of cabins nestled deep in forested areas. It was home to loggers and hermits, the ideal place to live among nature and escape the world. As far as hiding spots went, it was damn perfect. The homes were isolated enough that neighbors wouldn't hear the cries of a three-month-old baby, and Finn knew for a fact that several of the cabins were owned by a property agent who handled rentals through an internet site. Use a fake name, a bogus credit card, and you have a place to stay for a few weeks.

According to the investigator, Valerie hadn't rented any property using her card, but that didn't mean she wasn't in Holliday. She'd seduced a lab tech at the adoption clinic, for chrissake. She could've easily figured out a way to pay for a cabin without using her credit card.

"You can't come with us," Finn said, trying to keep the irritation from his voice.

Sarah's brown eyes flashed. "I don't believe this. You're actually keeping me away from—"

"I mean you *can't* come," he interrupted, running a hand through his hair. He shot a pointed look at her ankle. "You physically can't."

Sarah's gaze dropped, her mouth trembling as she stared at the electronic monitor clamped around her ankle. Her entire face crumpled in disappointment, sending a hot rush of pain to his gut.

With her lips quivering like that, he knew it was a matter of time before she started to cry, and so he quickly placed his hands on her slender waist and pulled her close. After a moment of hesitation, she sank into his embrace.

"I know you want to be there," he said, threading one hand through her silky dark hair. "And I wish to

God I could take you with us, but if that monitor starts beeping, the D.A. will be alerted and you'll be thrown back in jail. You won't be of any use to Lucy if you're behind bars, sweetheart."

"I know," she whispered. Pulling back, she locked her gaze with his. "Do you think she's there, in Holliday?"

"I don't know," he admitted. "This could be a total dead end. Valerie's credit card might have been stolen, or if she did use it, she might have just been stopping along. But if Lucy's there, we'll find her."

Parsons would probably kill him for taking the credit away from the federal agent, but Finn had no intention of involving the FBI during this search. He'd spoken to Jamie about it, and she'd agreed, warning him that Parsons would go in guns blazing. Since he had no desire to see Lucy—or hell, even Valerie—get hurt, Finn had opted to keep this road trip from the special agent. He and Anna would be taking one car, Jamie and Max would take the other, and the four of them would do this on their own. Holliday was a minuscule county, not even on the map, and with only forty or so houses in the area, they could be in and out of there before Parsons even figured out they were gone.

Finn just prayed his gut wasn't steering him in the wrong direction. He didn't want to waste manpower looking in the wrong place, but he couldn't ignore the information from Cole's P.I., either. If Lucy was in Holliday, he damn well planned on finding her.

"Will you call me the second you know?" Sarah asked, her hurt voice making his chest squeeze.

"The second I know," he echoed, stroking her hair. He gazed into her eyes, swallowing when he noticed that a new emotion had joined the angst and grief on her face. He saw a flicker of heat, even a burst of pride.

"You'll get her back for me, won't you, Finn?"

"Even if I die trying, sweetheart."

She searched his face once more, and then her lips were moving against his own as she kissed him so deeply, so passionately, he couldn't take a breath. She tasted like coffee and sugar and something distinctly Sarah. Her tongue pushed its way into his mouth and he was helpless to hide his immediate reaction. She let out a soft moan when she felt the hard ridge of his arousal against her belly, kissing him even harder.

His heart was slapping against his ribs when they finally pulled apart, and he almost didn't hear her as she whispered, "Don't."

"Don't what?" he asked gruffly.

"Die trying." She gave a little sigh. "I want Lucy back, but I don't want you to get hurt. Just…promise you'll be careful, okay?"

It was hard to speak through the monstrous lump in his throat. "I'll be careful." He swept his gaze over her one last time, smiling at her red, swollen lips, her silky smooth cheeks and delicate chin. "I have to go now. I'll call you when I know something."

As he left Sarah's house and walked toward the driveway, his chest was full of emotion. His mouth still tingled from that surprise kiss, the taste of Sarah imprinted there. It drove him mad, that she was right there in front of him, yet so out of reach. It had taken him four years to realize his mistakes, to grow up and become the man Sarah had wanted him to be back then.

Now that he was ready, *she* wasn't, and he had no idea how to change her mind.

Find her daughter, then worry about the rest.

It was a sobering thought, one he held on to as he hopped into the Jeep and drove away from Sarah's house.

Anna was waiting for him in the parking lot of the police station when he pulled up ten minutes later. He'd asked her to wait there, just in case Parsons was peeking out the window. According to Max, the agent was in Finn's office, preparing a statement for the press about the status of the investigation.

"Jamie and Max already left for Holliday," Anna said as she got into the Jeep. She unfolded a square of paper and handed it to him. "Jamie said they'd check all the houses she marked in blue. We're in charge of the red ones."

Finn glanced at the map, pleased to see there were only about two dozen red circles. The clock on the dash read twelve-fifteen. It would take about forty-five minutes to get to Holliday, where they'd have the entire day and night to dig around. His gaze dropped to Anna's feet, and he gave a pleased nod when he saw she'd changed into hiking boots as he'd requested. Some of those cabins required a trek and a half through the forest, which he wasn't particularly looking forward to.

Yesterday's rain was nowhere in sight as they set off in the direction of the highway. The sun was high in the sky, bright enough that Finn grabbed his aviator sunglasses from the cup holder and slipped them on his nose. He checked the rearview mirror, spotting the baby seat he'd taken from Sarah and buckled in the backseat. Was he placing too much hope on this? Maybe. But his hunches rarely steered him wrong, and from the moment Cole told him about the grocery purchase on Valerie's card, the nape of Finn's neck had been tingling.

"Okay," Anna said, her nose buried in the map. "The first house is right after the exit ramp, so don't miss the turnoff."

They didn't say much during the long drive. Finn was too tense. Too chock-full of adrenaline. He kept thinking of Sarah's anguished face when he told her that she couldn't come with him. He wished she could be here with him. He'd been wishing it for four years.

He slowed the Jeep when the exit for Holliday County came into view. Just as Anna had instructed, he turned right at the first turnoff, steering onto a dirt path that led to a sprawling ranch house in the distance. Ten seconds later, disappointment crashed into him, as he realized they'd struck out on the first try. Five towheaded children, ranging from toddler to preteen, were playing in the front yard, shrieking with delight as they dashed through an arch of water created by the lawn sprinkler. A woman with a big straw hat sat on the porch, reading a magazine.

Anna looked equally disappointed. "I don't think we'll find anything here."

Finn concurred, but they still had to be certain. Hopping out of the Jeep, they approached the porch, where they spent five minutes chatting with the woman in the straw hat, while Anna watched the children in the yard with faint longing in her eyes. They didn't linger long, just enough for Finn's gut to tell him that this perfect family wasn't aiding and abetting a kidnapper, and then they were off to the next house. And then another. And another.

It was nearly three o'clock when Anna crossed off yet another address on their map. They'd visited thirteen houses, and no Valerie or Lucy at any of them.

Jamie and Max were striking out, too, each phone call causing Finn's spirits to sink a little bit lower.

"Maybe she really did just pass through here," Anna said, sounding glum as they drove toward their next location.

"It's starting to feel that way," Finn confessed.

"Turn left there."

He followed her directions, and they ended up on yet another dirt path, this one winding several times before abruptly ending in front of an iron gate. The two halves of the metal barrier were chained together at the middle, a *No Trespassing* sign nailed to one of the wooden posts on each end of the gate. Beyond it, the terrain was rocky, surrounded by tall trees letting in flashes of sunlight through the thick leaves.

"Looks like we're walking," Finn remarked.

Anna grumbled under her breath as they got out of the car. "Well, hopefully we don't find ourselves facing down the barrel of a shotgun again. That guy at the last house was totally scary."

He grinned. "You could have taken him."

"Is that why you hid behind me? Because you knew I could take him?"

"Naah, I just forgot to bring my bulletproof vest," he kidded.

Laughing, she followed him into the trees. Finn kept his hand on the butt of the Beretta poking out of his holster, but he knew they probably wouldn't encounter any threats. So far, the visits had been harmless, except for the shotgun man who lectured them for trespassing.

The sun shone up above, making beads of sweat pop up on his forehead. Even with the shade of the trees, it was damn hot outside. They walked at a brisk pace, sidestepping fallen logs and the occasional poison ivy bush, until the trees thinned out and Finn glimpsed a small, A-frame cabin through the branches.

His instincts hummed.

"Stay behind me," he told Anna in a low voice.

She immediately fell back and he took the lead, keeping his gaze trained on the innocuous-looking cabin a few hundred yards away. The cabin had a tin roof and a narrow wraparound porch, the weathered logs at its exterior gleaming in the afternoon sun. There was no driveway, just yellow-green grass and broken lawn furniture. The sagging porch swing creaked as the breeze hit it.

The place looked abandoned, and with no car in sight, he doubted Valerie would have chosen this as her hideout. Walking through the forest with a three-month-old infant wailing in her arms? He couldn't picture Valerie having the patience for that, and he was about to tell Anna they should turn around when she suddenly hissed out a breath.

"There's someone at the window, boss."

He followed her gaze, instantly seeing what she had. A pale face in the window, unrecognizable from this far away. They picked up the pace, staying in the trees as they advanced on the cabin. The closer they got, the more excited he felt. There was definitely someone standing in the window. A woman, judging from the long hair. Long *black* hair.

Valerie.

"Stop," Finn ordered, pausing next to one of the thick redwood trunks.

From this point on, they would no longer have the cover of the trees. They would enter the clearing in front of the cabin, completely visible to the woman in the window. Finn was debating whether to run for the door when a baby's cry sliced through the air.

"Lucy," Anna whispered.

Finn let out a soft expletive. His fingers hovered over the butt of his gun, but he couldn't bring himself to draw the weapon. What if Valerie was armed, too? What if she freaked when she saw them and hurt herself or the baby?

"What do we do?" Anna demanded in a hushed voice. "Should we break down the door?"

"She'll see us coming before we could even make it to the door." Tension knotted around his muscles. "Okay. We walk up, slowly." He unholstered his weapon and gestured for Anna to do the same. "Follow my lead."

Finn uttered a silent prayer, then stepped away from the trees, his stride cautious. There was a flurry of movement in the window. Valerie had bolted away from it.

He took a breath. "Valerie!" he shouted. "It's Finn—I'm just here to talk!"

He and Anna approached the cabin, but he signaled for her to stop before she could climb the porch steps.

"Valerie, we're putting down our weapons, okay? We're not armed."

Although Anna looked reluctant, she mimicked his actions by placing her weapon on the grass, next to his.

Finn swore he saw the tattered curtain at the window move. "Valerie!" he shouted again. "Come out here. I just want to talk."

There was no response, no face in the window, and then a baby's distressed wails came from inside the house. Finn sprang to action, leaving his weapon on the grass as he charged to the door. He was prepared to kick it in, but a try at the doorknob and he realized it was unlocked.

He burst into the musty-smelling cabin and found the main room empty, but Lucy was still crying, the high-pitched shrieks pulsing from the back of the house. Finn took off toward the corridor, his heavy boots thudding against the weathered wood floor. He heard another cry, a muffled female curse, and skidded to a stop in front of the door at the end of the hall.

His heart jammed in his throat as his gaze registered everything. Valerie Matthews stood by a white-painted crib, clutching Sarah's daughter to her chest. Her raven hair was falling into a pair of wild gray eyes, which widened in shock and anger when she spotted Finn in the doorway.

"No!" she cried, her voice sizzling with fury. "I won't let you take her away from me, Finn!"

He took a cautious step forward, then halted when Valerie clutched the baby even tighter. "Valerie," he said softly. "Val, look at me."

Those silver eyes looked out of focus as they connected with his. "You can't take her, Finn."

To his shock, tears slid down her ivory-pale cheeks. Lucy opened her mouth and belted out another shriek. Valerie looked down at the baby as if she couldn't comprehend why the child would be crying.

"She's always crying," Valerie whispered. "She's always crying. Maybe she knows…" She stared at him in misery. "Do you think she knows I'm not her mother?"

Finn had no idea what to say. From the corner of his eye, he saw Anna entering the hallway, holding the gun he'd ordered her to drop. He gave an imperceptible shake of the head, silently ordering her to stay put.

This situation was too perilous. Valerie didn't look like she was going to hurt Lucy, but she was obviously distraught. She was shaking, crying even harder now, while the baby shrieked and wiggled in her arms.

"Valerie…why don't you put Lucy in the crib so you and I can have a little chat?"

Her jaw hardened. "Do you think I'm stupid? The second I put her down, you're going to shoot me!"

"I'm not going to shoot you." He raised both arms, then did a little spin. "I'm not armed. My gun is sitting outside on the grass. I don't want anyone to get hurt here, especially you or the baby."

She blinked rapidly, her face stained with her tears. "I know you probably think I've gone insane, but I had to take her, Finn. There's so much you don't know about—"

"I know Teresa is Lucy's biological mother."

Valerie gasped. "You do?"

He nodded.

"Then you understand why I had to do this!"

She shifted the baby so that Lucy's head rested on her shoulder, but that didn't abate the child's wails. Finn's temples were beginning to throb from those shrill noises.

"Lucy belongs with me," Valerie said, gently patting the baby's back in a soothing motion. "I'm her aunt. My little sister would want me to take care of her daughter. You understand, right, Finn?"

He swallowed. "I do understand. But Val…Lucy is Sarah's daughter now. She adopted—"

"She stole her from Teresa!" Valerie roared.

Evidently picking up on the anger vibrating from the body of the woman who held her, Lucy's cries kicked up another notch, the ear-splitting volume making both Finn and Valerie flinch.

"That nutcase knew Teresa was the birth mother!" Valerie went on. "That's why she killed her! So Teresa wouldn't take the baby back!"

Her growing agitation worried him, and he took a few more steps toward her. She growled at him and he halted again, speaking above Lucy's shrieks. "Sarah didn't kill your sister. And she didn't steal Lucy. Teresa gave up her legal rights, Val. She *gave* her baby away."

Valerie hiccupped, her hand moving to cup Lucy's downy head. That only got Lucy going even more, and the frustration swimming in Valerie's gray eyes grew. "Please stop crying," she begged the screaming, red-faced infant. "Just stop crying. You're safe, little girl. I'm here, baby."

Finn took her momentary state of distraction to make his move. He bounded across the room, ignoring Valerie's shocked gasp as he plucked the baby from her arms. With Lucy tucked against his chest like a football, he stepped away, temporarily losing the function of one eardrum as Lucy howled into it.

"Give her back!"

Valerie's enraged snarl had him hurrying to the doorway where Anna was waiting. As adrenaline coursed through his blood, he deposited Lucy into his deputy's arms and snapped, "Go! Get back to the Jeep."

Anna spun around without a word, reaching the end of the hall just as Valerie launched herself at Finn, nearly knocking him off his feet. Her fists pummeled into his chest, her tears soaking her face as she pounded at him for all she was worth, sobbing and yelling incoherently.

"How could you," she choked out. "How could—" she sobbed "—you do that? She's mine."

Finn grabbed hold of her fists and locked them between his hands. Valerie's heartfelt cries were even worse than Lucy's. In that brief moment, he actually saw the real Valerie Matthews. The daughter of the town drunk, the insecure, needy woman who had never caught a single break in life, whose sister had been taken away from her, whose only living relative had just been whisked out of this sad, dismal cabin.

"How could you," she whispered, her sobs mixed with quiet, unsteady pants.

With a sigh, Finn pulled her close, wrapped his arms around her, and listened to her weep.

Chapter 13

Sarah could make out the sound of a baby crying. Even in her dream, she recognized Lucy's wail, those little hiccups and the breathy wheezing noises at the tail end of each cry. *I'm coming,* she yelled in the darkness. *I'm coming, Lucy.*

The screams only grew louder, the darkness thicker. Panic spiraled through her and then her eyelids snapped open. She gasped for air, disoriented as her gaze darted around the room. She was in her bedroom. Sunlight streamed in through the open curtains. It was nearly four o'clock, according to the alarm clock. Finn had been gone for hours, and somehow, despite the terror and anticipation wreaking havoc on her body, she'd managed to fall asleep.

"Just a dream," she murmured to herself, waiting for her raging pulse to slow.

So why did she still hear her baby crying?

Fighting back tears, she stood up, wrapping the two ends of her long shawl around her. She was so cold. So damn afraid. The muffled sound of Lucy's cries echoed in her head, driving her absolutely insane.

"Sarah?"

Finn's voice.

She went still. She hadn't even heard him come in.

And Lucy's wails were still ringing in her brain, making her—oh God, they were coming from downstairs!

The oxygen left her lungs and her legs nearly collapsed beneath her. She wasn't imagining it. She could *hear* Lucy!

Tearing out of the room, she flew toward the staircase, disbelief and pure joy spinning inside her like a tornado. When she saw Finn at the bottom of the stairs, she let out a cry, then bounded down the steps and grabbed Lucy from Finn's outstretched hands.

"Oh, my God," she said through her tears. "Oh, my God, you found her."

She clung to her child, breathing in the sweet scent of shampoo and baby powder. The warm bundle squirmed in her arms, but she didn't ease her grip. She held Lucy tight as tears poured down her cheeks and sprinkled into Lucy's face. Lucy didn't seem to mind, though. Her distress faded, as if she realized she was exactly where she belonged and had no need to voice her displeasure any longer.

"Oh, my sweet baby," Sarah whispered.

Through a sheen of moisture, she saw Finn watching the reunion with a gentle smile on his rugged face. He looked happy and triumphant and relieved, and she found herself moving into the arms he opened, letting him envelop her and Lucy in his strong embrace. The feel of his hands running over the small of her back brought a rush of warmth. Even Lucy seemed to be enjoying the hug, letting out a jubilant gurgle.

"Thank you," Sarah said, lifting her head to meet his gorgeous blue eyes. "Thank you for bringing her home."

Raw emotion moved across his face. "It was my pleasure."

Swallowing, Sarah stepped out of his arms, still holding Lucy close. "Valerie?" she asked quietly.

He nodded. "She was hiding in a cabin in Holliday. Max and Anna took her to the station. She's charged with kidnapping."

Sarah didn't feel an ounce of sympathy. Valerie Matthews had stolen her child. It didn't make a difference if the woman was technically Lucy's aunt. Sarah knew she could never forgive Valerie for what she'd put her through. All those hours of worrying, crying, wondering if she'd ever see her child again. What Valerie had done was unforgivable.

"Do you...do you think she killed Teresa, too?" Sarah asked, holding her breath. If Valerie was the killer, that would make things so much easier, but to her disappointment, Finn shook his head.

"I don't think so. She has an alibi, but more than that, I think she's truly devastated about losing her sister. Teresa was the only family she had. That's why she took Lucy, because she no longer had her sister." He sighed. "Parsons is dealing with her, since the abduction is his case, as he continually likes to remind me. But when I spoke to him on the phone to tell him the news, he reminded me, not so nicely, I might add, that you're still charged with murder."

"And in five days, Gregory will get his indictment," Sarah said dully.

"Which means I need to step up my game and find the murderer," Finn answered, steely determination in his eyes.

She couldn't help but smile. "You haven't done enough already? You brought my daughter home."

"And now I'm going to make sure she stays home. With her mother."

Their gazes locked, and Sarah experienced a burst of longing. She wanted so badly to sink into his arms again. She wanted to kiss him again.

Obviously the relief talking. Just because Finn had kept his promise and brought Lucy home didn't mean she ought to open her heart to him. Her daughter was still her first priority, and letting Finn get close to Lucy, only to have him leave again, wouldn't be good for anyone.

Lucy opened her mouth and gave the cutest little yawn, her sleepy eyes causing Sarah to focus on the present. "I need to give her a bath and put her down to sleep," she said.

"And I need to get to the station. I want to be there when Parsons talks to Valerie."

They stood there at the foot of the stairs, each of them fidgeting. Sarah got the feeling he didn't want to leave. And she didn't *want* him to leave, yet she knew it was for the best. She was so extremely grateful to him for finding Lucy, and yes, maybe she was feeling those little sparks of longing, but right now, she needed to focus on her daughter. She could sift through her conflicting feelings for Finn later.

He seemed to be waiting for her to say something, and his shoulders sagged a bit when she didn't. "All right, I'd better go. I'll let you know what happens with Valerie."

Holding Lucy against her breast, Sarah followed him to the door. As he reached for the doorknob, she was the one hesitating this time.

"Do you want to come back for dinner?" she blurted out.

His hand stilled on the knob. The lopsided smile he gave her was utterly appealing. "Do you want me to?"

She managed a nod.

"Okay. What time?"

"We'll have to make it a late dinner. Give me a few hours, and maybe show up around eight-thirty? I'll whip up some pasta. I know you like steak, but I haven't been shopping for groceries since…since everything," she finished awkwardly.

"Pasta sounds great," he said gruffly. He moved his gaze to Lucy, another smile lifting his mouth. "I'm glad she's home. Take good care of her, Sarah."

"I will."

With a quiet goodbye, he left the house. Sarah locked up after him then headed toward the stairs. Lucy had fallen asleep in her arms, and a rush of tenderness flooded Sarah's belly as she stared down at her sleeping child.

Lucy was home.

Finn had brought her home.

Gently stroking Lucy's unbelievably soft cheek, Sarah walked upstairs, holding her beautiful daughter.

Finn stopped off at his house to shower and change after he left the police station, but didn't bother with a shave. He knew Sarah had a thing for his scruffy look, and right now, he needed every weapon in his arsenal to win her over. She was warming up to the idea. He'd seen it in her eyes earlier, when she'd invited him to dinner. He knew she was scared—he'd seen that on her face, too, but he planned on proving to her that she had no reason to be afraid.

He'd grown up these past few years, acknowledged the grave mistake he'd made when he'd walked out of Sarah's life. All he needed now was a chance. A chance to show her that everything could be different this time around.

He'd probably have a better shot at it if he found out who the hell had killed Teresa Donovan. As long as Sarah had this murder charge hanging over her head, she would be less open to the idea of accepting him back in her life. Why would she, if she would only be hauled off to jail?

He'd hoped that Valerie would help shed some light on that topic, but to his extreme frustration, she was refusing to talk. He and Parsons had attempted to question her, but gone was the woman who'd cried in Finn's arms only hours ago. The old Valerie had returned, with her hyperbolic sense of self-importance and that nasty sarcasm that never failed to annoy him. She'd coldly informed them that her lawyer would get her out of this mess, then crossed her arms and demanded a cup of coffee and something to eat, like a modern Marie Antoinette.

Finn planned on getting her alone tomorrow, maybe after Valerie's lawyer talked some sense into her. There was no way she was getting out of this "mess" unscathed. She'd kidnapped a child, for Pete's sake. Maybe once she got that through her head, he might get some answers from her about who may have killed her sister. She probably didn't even know, but Finn was at the point where he'd take all the assistance he could get, even if it came from Valerie Matthews.

He could think about all that tomorrow, though. Tonight he simply wanted to convince Sarah to give him a second chance.

After slipping into a clean pair of jeans and a black cable-knit sweater Sarah had given him years ago, he left his bedroom and headed downstairs, acutely aware of the complete lack of furniture or decoration in the main floor of his farmhouse. He hadn't grown up here—the house he'd shared with his mother had been sold years ago—but this farmhouse gave him the same sense of loneliness his childhood home had evoked. He'd bought this place hoping to build a life with Sarah. After she'd moved in, they had so many ideas about what to do with the place, how to renovate it, but within two months, Sarah got pregnant, and the only room they'd focused on was the nursery.

The nursery was still up there, across from the master bedroom on the second floor. He hadn't even cleaned it out, simply locked the door and forced himself to forget about what lay inside. Jason's crib. The sky-blue wallpaper and shelves of stuffed animals. It was all there, and in four years, he'd pretended none of it existed. Now, he felt a burst of hope as he remembered the pretty bedroom he and Sarah had labored on. He suddenly pictured Lucy inside of it, and his heart squeezed in his chest.

Way premature, man.

Right. He couldn't get ahead of himself. Sarah hadn't even agreed to date him, let alone move back in.

Still, he was whistling to himself as he slid into the Jeep and drove in the direction of Sarah's house. All the lights were on when he pulled into her driveway, but when he climbed the porch and knocked on the door, she didn't answer. He considered using the doorbell, but didn't want to wake Lucy if Sarah had just put her down. Instead, he let himself in and quietly called her name.

Again, no answer, but he knew she was home. Her purse was on the little credenza in the hall, as were her car keys. He almost raised his voice and called out again, then realized he knew exactly where she was.

Taking the stairs two at a time, he made his way to Lucy's nursery, pausing in front of the doorway. The room was dark, save for a Winnie the Pooh night-light plugged into the wall by the door. In the dim glow, he saw Sarah standing by Lucy's crib, her long hair falling over like a silky curtain as she gazed down at her child.

"Sarah," he murmured.

She jumped, spun around, then relaxed. "Hey," she whispered. "Talk quietly. She's sleeping."

Moving slowly so his boots wouldn't thud against the floor, he approached the crib and peered down, his chest becoming hot. Lucy was on her back, looking sweet and clean in a pink sleeper, her eyelids closed in slumber. A smile tugged at his mouth when he noticed that her bottom lip was sticking out in a little pout.

"She's beautiful," he said.

Sarah gave him a sidelong look. "I know, isn't she? I haven't been able to stop looking at her. I swear, I've been standing here for the past two hours, just watching her sleep." She suddenly gave a little gasp. "Shoot, dinner!"

The baby stirred at her mother's outburst, and Sarah quickly lowered her voice before continuing. "Finn, I didn't even start dinner yet. I was—"

"Watching your daughter sleep," he finished with a faint smile. "No worries. We'll fix something together."

Not that he was even hungry. His stomach had been in a state of clenched anxiety since the dinner invitation. Probably not the most masculine reaction, but he couldn't get rid of those damned butterflies fluttering around in his gut. This was the closest he'd come in years to getting Sarah back, and a part of him desperately feared he'd blow it.

Sarah reached down to stroke her daughter's cheek, then tucked the thin blanket up to Lucy's chin. "Okay, let's go downstairs and—"

A loud beep broke the peaceful silence, followed by three more sharp chimes that had Finn ushering Sarah out of the nursery. He closed the door behind them, then peered down at her ankle with a frown. The bracelet displayed a red light, which blinked in time with the beeps.

Sarah's lips tightened. "I forgot to change the batteries."

The electronic monitor was a reminder of yet another obstacle that stood in his path, and Finn resisted the urge to put his fist through the wall. Lord, she didn't deserve this, being kept on a damn leash while the real murderer roamed the streets, free to do whatever the hell he wanted.

Trying to hide his anger, Finn took her arm and led her to the bedroom. "Do you still keep batteries in your nightstand?" he asked.

She laughed. "You remember that?"

He was already yanking open the top drawer. "You used to keep everything in there. Batteries, spare keys, pencils, Band-Aids—I never understood why you needed all that stuff so close at hand. That's what hall closets are for."

"A nightstand is as good a place as any," she protested.

"Whatever you say, sweetheart." He rummaged around in the drawer, which was filled to the gills, until he finally found an unopened pack of batteries. "Sit down, I'll do it for you," he said over his shoulder.

He heard the bedspread rustle as she lowered herself on the mattress. Tearing open the cardboard, he took out two fresh batteries and knelt on the floor in front of Sarah. She seemed to hesitate, then raised her foot. She'd changed into a pair of knee-length black leggings and an oversize green sweater that hung down to her knees. She wasn't wearing any socks, and her pale pink toenails made his mouth go dry. So did the sight of her sleek calves and delicate feet.

When he placed her foot in his lap, her breath hitched. "Are my hands too cold?" he asked gruffly.

She slowly shook her head. "No."

Finn swallowed in order to clear the sawdust from his mouth. Then he popped open the small compartment on the ankle bracelet, removed the dead batteries and slid in the new ones. The second he snapped them in place, the beeping stopped and the red light went off, but for the life of him, he couldn't let go of her foot.

Her skin was hot to the touch. When he moved his gaze up her body, he noticed her nipples poking against the front of her sweater. The material was so thin, he could tell she wasn't wearing a bra, and his mouth promptly turned into a desert once more.

Unable to stop himself, he caressed the arch of her foot.

"Finn," she breathed. "What…what are you doing?"

He didn't answer. Wrapping his fingers around her other ankle, he caressed her smooth skin, then dragged both hands up to her knees, her thighs, her waist, her flat belly. He could see her pulse throbbing in her graceful neck, but the expression on her beautiful face was encouraging. He saw anticipation, heat.

He moved his hands higher, resting them just below the swell of her breasts. He waited, met her eyes again, and glimpsed only desire. Emboldened, he cupped her breasts over her sweater, squeezing the full mounds and eliciting a shaky sigh from her lush mouth.

"Finn," she murmured again.

"Tell me to stop," he murmured back. "Say it, and I'll walk out of this room."

Her mouth opened. He waited, praying she didn't say those words.

"Touch me," she whispered.

Joy shot through him. Before she could change her mind, he tangled one hand through her hair and tugged her toward him, kissing her hard and deep. She gasped against his mouth, then relaxed, parting her lips so he could slide his tongue inside, so he could lick and explore and drink her in.

Every muscle in his body was coiled tight. His groin throbbed, the erection straining against his zipper harder and more painful than ever. He'd been with a few women since he and Sarah broke up, but none of them had inspired this primal reaction inside of him. None of them had made his heart pound and made him hungry with desire. Sarah was the only one who did that, the only one who could satisfy his appetite, his need.

As their tongues danced and dueled, he bunched up the hem of her sweater and pulled the material over her head. Her bare breasts gleamed in the patch of moonlight shining through the open window. He went dizzy for a second, lost in the incredible vision of those mouthwatering mounds and the tight pink nipples begging for his attention.

When he lowered his mouth and sucked one rigid bud deep in his mouth, Sarah moaned, then cupped his head and brought him closer, welcoming him, trapping him. He circled each bud with his tongue. Sucking, licking, while his hand moved between her legs to rub her over her leggings.

She gasped, arching off the bed, and when her thighs parted slightly, he cupped her fully, grinding his palm over her hot core.

"Let's get these clothes off," he rasped, already moving to his waistband.

Sarah looked as anxious as he felt, and soon their clothes were being peeled off and thrown aside, until they were both naked and stumbling onto the bed. He covered her body with his, groaning at the feel of her soft curves beneath him, her peaked nipples rubbing against his chest.

Burying his face in the crook of her neck, he kissed the soft flesh there, gliding his mouth down to her collarbone then resuming his ministrations on her breasts. Her fingernails dug into his shoulders, her legs scissoring relentlessly as she moaned in pleasure.

"I've missed this," she whispered.

"Me, too," he said hoarsely.

He sucked her nipple deep in his mouth, then blew a stream of air over it, enjoying the way it hardened, the way she sighed. Turning his attention to the other breast, he slid his hand between their bodies and teased her core, finding her damp and swollen and drenched with desire. He stroked, explored, then pushed his finger inside of her, nearly losing control when her inner muscles clamped around it.

Lord, he could touch her for hours. Days. And never grow tired. He dipped his head and kissed her again, and when she swept her tongue over his bottom lip, he groaned. Knew without a doubt that this was where he belonged. This was who he belonged with. No, who he belonged *to*. He was Sarah's, always had been, always would be.

"You're teasing me," she choked out as he drew another finger into the fold.

He shot her a heavy-lidded look. "Are you complaining?"

"No, just contemplating payback."

"Payba—"

Before he could finish, she had her palms on his chest and was pushing him off her. He rolled onto his back, his pulse kicking up a notch when Sarah straddled him. She leaned forward, her thick dark hair cascading over one shoulder and tickling the hair on his chest. When her warm mouth pressed a kiss on his scorching skin, he almost lost it again. Breathing through his nose, he clenched his fists at his sides, forcing himself not to move.

Sarah's eager hands and wicked tongue had him seeing through a red haze of arousal. She placed openmouthed kisses on his chest, her tongue darting out to taste one flat nipple. His world began to spin, potent desire sizzling his nerve endings. He forgot how to breathe as she moved down his body, getting perilously close to the erection threatening to turn this mind-blowing encounter into total embarrassment.

Gritting his teeth, he allowed her mouth to close over

his tip. Her tongue to trace a path along his shaft. One soft lick, two—and then he gently grabbed hold of her hair and yanked her up.

"I'm too close," he murmured.

A playful smile lifted the corners of her lush mouth. "What happened to the famous Finnegan endurance?"

He choked on a laugh. "It took one look at your sexy naked body and ran out the door."

Her responding laughter only made him harder. He loved the way she laughed, that melodic, throaty lilt. It had been far too long since he'd seen the amusement dancing in her eyes.

Sarah climbed off him, eliciting a jolt of disappointment. But then he realized she was turning to her trusty nightstand, and anticipation kicked in. She found a condom and handed it to him, and his damn hands shook as he put the thing on. He felt like a teenager again, out of control, nervous that he might screw this up.

But Sarah wasn't complaining as he covered her body again and slid into her in one powerful thrust. Moaning, she hooked her legs around his waist, the heels of her feet digging into his buttocks as he moved inside of her. The feel of her tight heat surrounding him made him groan in sheer desperation. It wasn't enough. He needed more. Needed to be deeper.

Their mouths fused together, tongues swirling in a hot, reckless kiss as he quickened his pace. He thrust into her, over and over, harder, faster, until a wild cry escaped her lips and she shouted his name. When she moaned a fervent *Yes* and shuddered beneath him, he toppled right over the edge.

Shards of pleasure assaulted his body, sizzling down his spine and filling his groin. With a hoarse groan, he let go, letting release take over, his body shaking and throbbing from the unbelievable sensations.

When he finally crashed back to earth, he heard Sarah laughing again, the beautiful sound tickling his chest. Cranking open his eyes, he peered down at her and muttered, "Something funny?"

She wrapped her arms around his damp back and pressed a kiss to his shoulder. "Nope. Not funny, just amazing."

Unable to let her go, he rolled them over so that he was on his back, Sarah's head resting against his chest. His heart continued to pound, every muscle in his body contracting and throbbing with lingering pleasure.

As he lay there holding Sarah, sated beyond belief, warmed by love and emotion, he couldn't stop his next words from slipping out of his mouth.

"Will you give me another chance?"

Chapter 14

Leave it to Finn to take the most incredible sexual afterglow and turn it into thick, throat-clogging tension. Sarah slid up and leaned against the headboard, the pleasure coursing through her body transforming into a dull ache of pain. Why did he have to push this? She'd thought that sex would be enough for him, but Finn was never satisfied with halfway. He always wanted it all.

Not that she'd slept with him to make him forget his desire to get back together. She'd wanted him. *Craved* him, and she couldn't deny that this man still had incredible power over her. He made her body sing, he made her feel alive.

But he also had the power to destroy her.

"Did you hear me?" he asked in a rough voice.

She sighed. "Yeah, I did. I just don't know what to say to that, Finn."

Fully naked, he got up and picked his boxers off

the floor, quickly slipping them up to his trim waist. She couldn't wrench her gaze away from his spectacular body, his muscular thighs, washboard stomach, the dusting of dark hair on his sleek chest. With his black hair messed up from their lovemaking and the stubble dotting his strong jaw, he looked rugged and sexy and unbelievably appealing. She'd always been a sucker for his scruffy look.

The expression in his eyes made him appear more dangerous than usual, a glimmer of anger and disbelief, directed at her. "You could say yes," he finally replied. "You could agree to give us a second chance."

Frustration crept up her throat. "I already told you before, this isn't just about us anymore. I have Lucy to think about now."

He looked wounded. "Do you think I would ever hurt her?"

"Not intentionally," she murmured. "But…I just don't want her depending on you, or falling in love with you, only to have you walk out if things don't work out between us."

He moved to the foot of the bed, curling his fingers over the wooden bed frame. "Who says it won't work out?" His features creased. "I don't remember you being a pessimist."

"I'm realistic," she snapped, suddenly growing annoyed with all of this. She hopped off the bed and searched for her underwear, finding her panties under the bed and her sweater hanging over an open dresser drawer. In their passion, they'd thrown items of clothing all over the place, and it only irritated her more as she gathered up the garments and got dressed. She always seemed to lose control when Finn was around.

"You're scared," he corrected, bending down to pick up his jeans.

The anger in the air hissed and crackled as they each dressed in a rush, as if the cotton and denim and other materials could protect them from the tension brewing between them.

"I understand why," he went on, looking shamefaced. "I broke your trust when I walked out on you, but the only way I can prove to you that I've changed is if you give me another chance. If you take a leap of faith and open your heart to me again."

She swallowed. "I don't know if I can."

"Then why am I even here?" he shot back.

She stared into his eyes and saw the dissatisfaction boiling there. He was right. Why *was* he here? Why had she allowed him to make love to her, why was she willing to give him her body, but not her heart?

Because he already broke it once.

"I love you, Sarah."

His quiet voice pierced right into her heart and made it ache.

"I want to be with you," he went on, his voice hoarse. "But not as an occasional lover, someone you sleep with whenever it tickles your fancy. I want a relationship with you."

Tears stung her eyes. A part of her wanted to throw herself into his arms and tell him that she loved him too, but those three frightening words got stuck in her throat like a wad of gum. She couldn't stop thinking about the last time she'd said those words, when she'd been curled up on their kitchen floor, pleading with him to stay.

"I don't know if I can give you what you want," she

whispered. "I can't make a decision like this on the spot. I need…time."

His jaw stiffened. "So you can think in circles and come up with reasons why we shouldn't be together? I can't sit around while you decide if I'm worth loving again. Either you love me, or you don't. Either you want to try again, or you don't."

"You're not being fair," she protested. "Why does everything have to be so black and white with you?"

"Because in this case, there's no gray. I'm in love with you, sweetheart. I want to be with you and show you I've changed. So either you're willing to take the chance, or you're not."

Silence stretched between them, an impassable chasm Sarah couldn't bridge. Everything he said made sense. If things were to work out between them, she *had* to take that chance. But fear was holding her back. No matter how hard she tried, she couldn't swallow down the terror coating her throat.

"Move back in with me," Finn said suddenly.

Her eyes went wide. "What?"

"Let's start over, Sarah. Live together again. There's even a nursery for Lucy."

Panic shuddered through her. "I…I can't. This is too fast for me, Finn. I can't make any of these decisions right now."

His expression clouded. "No, you're just too scared to make them."

She clenched her teeth, so hard her jaw started to hurt. "And you think dropping ultimatums is going to make me less afraid? God, Finn, I'm only asking for time. Why does everything have to be done your way, when *you* want it?"

"Because we've wasted enough time already," he

said hoarsely. "Because I love you and want to be with you." He met her eyes. "The question is—do *you* want to be with *me?*"

That same rope of fear wrapped around her throat. "I…"

Her voice trailed, and Finn sucked in a harsh breath. "I'll take that as a no then."

She made one final attempt to make him see reason. "Finn, come on, don't be like this."

His shoulders were stiff as he headed for the door. "I'm sorry, Sarah, but I won't wait around for you to decide if you love me or not."

She gaped at him. Why was he being so damn difficult? This had nothing to do with love, and he knew it. It was about trust. Faith. And yes, fear. But how could he blame her for being afraid after what happened the last time?

Her body tightened with irritation. Fine, if he was going to be a total jerk about this, she wasn't about to indulge him.

"Then go," she said coolly. "Because there's no point in you sticking around, right?"

His blue eyes flickered with hesitation, then hardened in resolve. "No, I guess there isn't."

And then he walked out the door.

It wasn't until eleven o'clock the next morning that Finn managed to get Valerie Matthews alone. She'd been with her lawyer for the past two hours, a man from the firm where Valerie worked as the office manager. Finn had loitered in the hall the entire time, waiting for his chance, which finally came when Valerie's attorney left to get himself and his client some lunch. Finn ducked into the neighboring interrogation room, waited until the man's footsteps retreated, then slid out and entered Valerie's room.

She scowled when he came in. "I have nothing to say to you, Finnegan."

"I don't suppose you do," he said pleasantly. "But I've got a lot to say to you."

He sat across from her, and for a moment, he didn't see Valerie, but Sarah. He remembered how distraught Sarah had been when he'd questioned her, how hurt. It almost thawed the icy band around his heart, the pain that had plagued him since he'd left Sarah's house last night.

He probably shouldn't have given her an ultimatum. He regretted it now, but at the time, he'd been too annoyed to think straight. Not even the incredible sex they'd shared had managed to convince her to let him back in. He'd already saved her child, and now he was racing to find the killer in order to clear her name. He wasn't sure what else he could do to prove to her that he truly loved her, that he'd genuinely changed.

Shoving away the bitterness, he focused on Valerie, deciding to go for the blunt approach. "You're going to jail, Val. Whatever your lawyer has been telling you, there's no way you're walking away from this without jail time."

Her gray eyes flashed. "You're a small-town sheriff. What do you know?"

"I know that no jury is going to buy a temporary insanity plea, or whatever your lawyer will have you say." He clasped his hands together. "You planned the kidnapping. You had a cabin ready—my deputies have been going through the place and informed me that you stocked up on supplies. This has premeditation written all over it. You're going to jail."

Some of her confidence chipped away. "I won't."

"Sure you will." He leaned back in his chair, as if he had all the time in the world, when in reality, a ticking clock was going off in his head. Four days. Gregory was taking Sarah's case to the grand jury in four days, unless Finn found a way to stop him.

"But your sentence might be reduced—if you're willing to cooperate."

She raised a brow. "Cooperate how? What information could I possibly have that will help you?"

"You can tell me who killed your sister, for starters."

Pain exploded in her eyes. "Why on earth would I know who killed Teresa?"

Damn. Finn hid his disappointment as he stared into her shocked face. Just as he'd suspected, Valerie obviously had no idea who killed Teresa. But maybe she could still offer something of use to him.

"You two were close," he pressed. "She must have told you she was sleeping around on Cole. So tell me, who else was she involved with? We know about Ian Macintosh and Parker Smith, but there were more men."

Valerie's expression went shuttered and a spark of triumph lit Finn's body. Bingo. She definitely knew something about *that* particular subject.

"My sister was misunderstood," Valerie finally replied, her voice cool. "She only cheated on Cole because he neglected her. He was never here."

Finn waved a dismissive hand. "I'm not interested in her motives. Just names." When Valerie didn't answer, he hardened his tone. "Give me a name."

Her throat dipped as she swallowed. "I don't know who she was involved with."

"That's bull. Teresa told you everything."

"Not everything," Valerie muttered.

Sensing he'd hit a nerve, he instantly pounced on the opening she'd given him. "You must have been furious when you found out she had a kid and gave it up for adoption. When did she tell you about it?"

"She didn't," Valerie corrected, then snapped her mouth shut as she realized what she'd said.

Finn raised his eyebrows. "If she didn't tell you, how did you learn about Lucy?"

The resolve in Valerie's eyes crumbled. "A medical bill came in the mail," she admitted. "It was under my name, charging me for a few tests that weren't covered by my insurance. Only problem was, I never underwent any tests, especially from a hospital in Raleigh. So I called them, and was informed that I gave birth to a baby girl." She shook her head, incredulous. "I immediately put two and two together and realized what she'd done."

"So you seduced some poor guy at the adoption clinic to see who adopted your sister's baby," Finn finished. He cocked his head. "What else did you figure out?"

"What do you mean?" she mumbled.

"Do you know who the father is?" Valerie went quiet, triggering Finn's inner alarm system. "You do, don't you? Who is it, Val? Who did Teresa conceive that baby with?"

Her lips were set in a tight line. "I have no idea what you're talking about."

Anger simmered in his stomach. "Don't play games, Valerie. I promise you, if you give me the information I'm asking for, I will personally go to the judge and plead for a lighter sentence on your behalf."

Valerie's reluctance was palpable, but he also witnessed a glimmer of optimism. She knew he was a man of his word. He'd proven that to her by working furiously to solve her sister's murder, no matter how much he'd despised Teresa. He followed every lead, every shred of evidence, even when it led to people he cared about, people he longed to protect.

"I'll discuss it with my lawyer," Valerie finally said.

He ignored the crushing disappointment. "Get back to me after you've done that, then. But time is of the essence, Val. I can't solve your sister's murder unless I have every detail available to me."

"You already solved it," she shot back. "Sarah Connelly did it, and I hope she rots in hell."

"Sarah didn't kill anyone," he said coldly. "Which means there's still a killer on the loose. If you want vengeance for Teresa, I suggest you help this investigation rather than hinder it."

He decided to leave that as his parting words. Scraping back his chair, he got to his feet, just as a knock rapped against the door and Max poked his head into the room. Shifting awkwardly, the deputy lifted the bright yellow mug in his hand and said, "I brought Ms. Matthews the coffee she asked for."

Finn stifled a sigh. He shouldn't be surprised that Valerie was sending his deputy out to fill her drink orders. That woman had more nerve than most people.

As Max walked to the table and handed Valerie the cup, Finn gave her one last pointed look, then left the room and headed for his office. He was annoyed to find Parsons behind his desk, reading over the report Anna had typed up about yesterday's rescue.

Parsons lifted his head when Finn came in. "I thought I made myself clear about keeping me updated on all leads relating to the abduction."

"There was no time," Finn lied. "Cole Donovan's P.I.

called me about the gas station receipt from Holliday
while you and Agent Bradley were interviewing Valerie's coworkers. I didn't want to interrupt you, I figured it would be a false alarm anyway, so I decided to
take my deputies."

Parsons saw right through the fabrication. "You decided to take the credit, you mean." The agent glared at
him. "I'm sick and tired of your unprofessional attitude,
Finnegan. And just so you know, I've been in constant
contact with Mayor Williams and I've made it clear to
him where I stand in regard to your badge."

"Whisper whatever you want into the mayor's ear.
The people of Serenade know who they voted for." Finn
stepped forward. "Now if you'll excuse me, I need to
go over some files, and I believe you're in my chair."

Although he didn't look at all pleased, Parsons re-
linquished the seat, tucking a file folder under his arm.
"I'll be working at Deputy Patton's desk. I'm writing
up a report for my supervisor about the abduction."

"Make sure you mention the part about me finding
the baby," Finn couldn't help but bite out.

Parsons stalked out without another word, as Finn
grinned to himself. Totally juvenile, maybe, but he
liked ruffling Parsons's feathers. The guy was a nar-
row-minded ass.

Settling in his chair, Finn unlocked the top drawer
of the desk and pulled out the folder containing the interviews he and his deputies had conducted after Teresa
was killed. He retrieved the first sheet, the statement
from Parker Smith. Smith was the young bartender
Teresa had slept with, the only one whose name she'd
revealed to Cole. Five minutes later, Finn reached for
the next interview. He read each one carefully, trying to
see if he'd missed something, but by the time he closed

the folder, he hadn't learned anything new. Everyone they'd spoken to claimed to have heard Teresa bragging about her lovers, but not one person had a name to back it up with.

But Finn was certain one of those mysterious men was the key to everything. He was particularly interested in Lucy's biological father, but unless Teresa rose from the dead and spilled her carnal secrets, he had no clue how to uncover the identities of her lovers.

Glancing at the clock on his screen saver, he noticed it was past noon. He'd been reading for almost an hour, and now his stomach growled, reminding him he hadn't eaten all day. When he'd woken up this morning, his appetite had been nonexistent. There had been a painful rock in his stomach since he'd left Sarah's last night.

Four years ago, she'd begged him to stay.

Last night, she'd told him to leave.

And like the idiot he was, he'd walked out that door for a second time. Why hadn't he stayed and tried to make her see how sincere he was?

She's too scared to see it.

He released a breath, knowing it was the truth. Sarah was afraid of getting hurt again. And worse, having Lucy get hurt in the process. He knew her resistance to a relationship with him had a lot to do with the fact that she was a mother now, but he had no idea how to convince her that he would never leave her—or Lucy. He was already madly in love with that baby girl. And he was madly in love with her mother, too.

He just wished Sarah could trust him enough to believe it.

"We need an ambulance!"

The shrill shout jolted Finn from his thoughts.

What the hell?

Scrambling to his feet, he raced out of the office, slamming into Parsons in the bull pen. Both men exchanged a puzzled look, as Parsons said, "What is going on?"

The two men hurried toward the commotion, flying into the corridor at the same time Anna and Max skidded to a stop. Both deputies looked shocked and confused, and all eyes turned to the open door of the interrogation room Finn had left Valerie in.

He rushed to the doorway, his body going cold when he saw Robert McNeil, Valerie's attorney, down on the floor, bending over his client. McNeil looked up with frantic eyes. "Call the paramedics!" he exclaimed. "She's not breathing. I came back with lunch and found her on the floor—Jesus Christ, why weren't any of you people watching her?"

Sucking in a gulp of oxygen, Finn burst into the room and joined McNeil on the floor, where Valerie lay motionless. Her eyes were closed and her face was paler than snow, contrasting with the black hair fanned out beneath her. It was like Teresa Donovan all over again, except this time there was no blood, no sign to indicate what had happened to Valerie.

Finn shrugged off the attorney's shaking hands and lowered his head over Valerie, listening carefully. McNeil was right, she wasn't breathing. As dread snaked up his spine and chilled his chest, he placed two fingers on her neck and checked for a pulse.

Nothing.

No pulse.

Valerie was dead.

Chapter 15

Finn was stunned speechless as he staggered to his feet. He couldn't bring himself to look at Valerie's lifeless body. She was dead. But how? Why? He'd spoken to her only an hour ago, and she hadn't exhibited any signs of…well, of *going to die soon*. Was it a heart attack? A seizure?

His brain was running a million miles a second as he stepped into the hallway, where Parsons, Max and Anna waited, staring at him in shock.

"What's going on?" Anna asked in bewilderment.

"Valerie's dead."

Both Anna and Max gasped, while Parsons gave him his trademark scowl. "What the hell are you talking about, Finnegan? I spoke to her an hour ago."

"So did I." He raked his fingers through his hair. "And now she's dead. Anna, call the coroner, tell him to get over here ASAP. We need to find out what happened to her."

Anna rushed off with a word, nearly colliding with Parsons's colleague, Agent Andrews, in the doorway. The blonde federal agent apologized to the deputy, then hurried toward the three men, a sheet of paper clutched in her hand.

"Sir," she said to Parsons, her tone urgent. "I just—"

"Not now, Charlene," he snapped. "We have a situation here."

The woman protested, but Parsons was already turning to glare at Finn. "Who saw Matthews?" he demanded. "Who went in to talk to her today?"

Finn frowned. "Do you think she was killed?"

"I'm not ruling anything out." Parsons swore loudly. "I find it mighty suspicious that she dropped dead an hour after I accused her of having an accomplice."

Finn faltered. Parsons had accused her of that? He suddenly recalled his own chat with Valerie, his demand that she give up the names of Teresa's lovers. Parsons's accomplice theory wasn't that far from his own. For all Finn knew, Valerie *had* been working with someone—her sister's lover, perhaps.

He glanced through the open doorway, flinching at the sight of McNeil doing chest compressions on Valerie. The thin man looked shell-shocked as he counted softly to himself. It wasn't every day a lawyer found his client dead on the floor, and Finn suspected McNeil was in shock, judging from his glazed eyes.

He was also potentially destroying evidence. Jumping to action, Finn strode back into the room and laid a gentle hand on McNeil's shoulder. "She's gone," he said in a low voice. "You need to step away now, Mr. McNeil. The coroner works right across the street and will be here any second."

When the lawyer seemed reluctant, Finn added, "This is a possible crime scene. You need to step away."

Removing his hands from Valerie Matthews's chest, McNeil allowed Finn to help him to his feet. "Why don't you fix yourself a cup of coffee and sit down in the bull pen?" Finn suggested. "Someone will come and talk to you soon."

The lawyer walked away, looking numb.

Finn turned back to Parsons, picking up where they left off. "Okay, you and I were both in to see her. McNeil. Anna brought her a glass of water this morning."

"I brought her coffee after you spoke to her," Max piped up.

"Anyone else?" Parsons barked.

"Sir," Agent Andrews began, still clutching her paper. "I have—"

"Not now, Andrews," he cut in. "Who else was in that room?"

"Nobody," Finn said flatly.

"I guess Dr. Bennett could have seen her on his way to your office," Max offered. "Maybe he went in and—"

"Bennett?" Finn said sharply. "What are you talking about?"

Max looked confused. "I saw him in the lobby. He said he was coming to speak to you, so I told him to go on back to your office."

Finn's body stiffened. "The doc never came to see me, Max."

"What? But he said—"

"Can you people just listen to me?" came a piercing female voice.

Finn gaped at the petite blonde who'd yelled at them,

noticing for the first time just how panic-stricken she looked. And she was holding on to that piece of paper as if it contained state secrets or something.

"If you'd all just quit ignoring me, I might be able to shed some light on this situation," Agent Andrews said stiffly.

Parsons had the decency to look repentant. "What is it?"

"I followed up with Walter Brown like you asked me to." She turned to Finn, adding, "The man who hosted the party in Grayden, his gun was stolen? Anyway, he gave me a list of the people at the party, the ones from Serenade."

She shoved the paper in Finn's hands. "Most of them were older men who worked at the paper mill with Brown and didn't have any connection to Teresa. But look at the second-to-last name."

Finn stared at the neatly handwritten list, his eyes narrowing when he saw what she indicated. Dr. Travis Bennett.

"He was at that party the night the murder weapon was stolen?" Finn demanded.

Andrews nodded. "And get this, Brown remembers giving Bennett a tour of the house, a tour that included the study, where Brown showed Bennett the gun. Bennett even admired it, said he wished he had one of his own."

"Son of a bitch," Finn muttered.

Travis Bennett had attended Brown's party, the same night Brown's gun was stolen. And Bennett had been here just now, claiming he'd come to see the sheriff—yet he never found his way to Finn's office.

"Who's this Bennett?" Parsons demanded, furrowing his pale eyebrows. "The name never came up in the case files."

"Because there was no reason to connect him to any of this," Finn replied. "Travis runs the clinic, you probably walked by it when you were at the lab—it's in the same build—" Finn spit out a curse.

Bennett's clinic was in the same building as the lab. The lab where the trace evidence from the Donovan crime scene had been stored. The hair found next to Teresa's body, the fingerprint on the coffee table. When the tech had run the evidence, Sarah's DNA and fingerprint had been flagged.

"He framed her," Finn mumbled. "He switched the results. He must have gotten into Tom's computer and somehow changed the real results, so that Sarah's DNA, which was already in the system from that stupid high school project, would pop up."

"What are you muttering about?" Parsons grumbled.

"Or…or he could have switched the samples," Finn realized, growing sicker by the second. "He's her doctor—he could easily get her DNA, a fingerprint, and pin the murder on her."

"Finnegan," Parsons said sharply. "Fill us in here."

Finn rubbed the sudden ache in his temples. "I think Bennett framed Sarah for Teresa's murder. He must have been one of Teresa's lovers."

"That's a pretty big assumption," Parsons retorted.

"It makes sense. Bennett had access to the crime scene evidence, he could have easily tampered with the results. And he had opportunity to steal the murder weapon from Brown's house." He cursed. "And I think you were right—Valerie had an accomplice. It must have been Bennett, and he killed her to shut her up."

"Unless she died of natural causes," Parsons pointed out.

"She didn't," came a grim voice.

Len Kirsch, the coroner, briskly exited the interrogation room, unsnapping a pair of white gloves from his hands. Finn hadn't even seen the man arrive, but then again, his mind had been somewhere else.

"I believe Ms. Matthews suffocated to death," Kirsch announced, tucking the gloves in his medical bag. "I found petechial hemorrhages in her eyes, which is a sign of—"

"Petechial what?" Finn interrupted.

"Hemorrhages," the coroner repeated. "They're tiny red spots caused by areas of bleeding. It's usually indicative of suffocation."

Finn wrinkled his brow. "So she was smothered to death?"

Kirsch shook his head. "I'll run tests at the lab, but I don't think so. It looks like an internal suffocation, maybe induced by a drug. I found a small pinprick on the right side of her neck. I think she may have been injected with something." He clicked his tongue. "Most likely phenobarbital—it's used in physician-assisted euthanasia, stops the breathing reflex and causes death by suffocation."

The word *physician* stayed in Finn's mind. Bennett would have access to drugs like that. And Bennett had been here, less than an hour ago, without visiting Finn's office like he'd told Max.

"Damn, Finnegan, I think you're right," Parsons said in a grudging tone. He turned to Andrews. "Take Bradley and go to Bennett's office, try to bring him in without a fight. Say we just need to ask him a few questions and—"

"He won't be there," Finn interrupted, a sick feeling creeping up his chest.

Parsons frowned. "You think he skipped town already?"

"No." He swallowed down the bile lining his throat. "I think he's going to tie up loose ends. He's going after Sarah."

When the doorbell rang, Sarah experienced both a burst of joy and a pang of dread. She knew it must be Finn, here to deliver news about Valerie's questioning, but a part of her was terrified to look into his eyes and see that dull expression he'd donned yesterday. She knew she'd hurt him by refusing to jump headfirst into a relationship with him, but she wished he could see where she was coming from. They had so much baggage, she and Finn, a rocky history punctuated by him abandoning her in her darkest hour.

He'd accused her of being scared—well, of course she was scared! Not only of getting her heart broken again, but of letting her daughter grow used to Finn as a father figure. If he could have just offered to take things slow, really slow, she might have given him that chance he'd asked for. But with Finn, it was always all or nothing.

And so he'd forced her hand, pushed her into a decision she wasn't ready to make, and as a result, got the answer he hadn't been looking for.

With a sigh, she picked the baby monitor off the kitchen counter and headed to the front door. Lucy was sound asleep upstairs, after the busy morning they'd had in the backyard. They'd enjoyed the sunshine, Lucy wiggling around on a flannel blanket while Sarah just lay there, staring at her daughter, afraid to take her eyes off her for even a second.

The doorbell chimed once more, and when she opened the front door, she was startled to see Travis Bennett on her porch. "Travis? What are you doing here?"

"Can I come in?" he asked.

She hesitated for a moment, bothered by his appearance. He was normally perfectly kempt, his suits starched and pressed, not a hair on his head out of place. Right now, though, he looked extremely agitated. His tie was off-kilter, his sleeves rolled up haphazardly, and nervous sparks flickered in his dark eyes.

"Are you okay?" she asked cautiously.

He shifted in his feet. "Not really."

Never one to turn away a friend in need, she opened the door wider and gestured for him to come in. It wasn't until he stepped inside that she noticed he was holding something at his side. A large metal can.

She furrowed her brow. "What is that?" Her eyes narrowed as she stared at his hand. "Is that a *gas* can? What's going on, Travis? Why did you come here?"

"I'm here for my daughter."

Sarah's mouth fell open. "What?"

His eyes were wild as he repeated his statement. "I'm here for my daughter. Lucy."

She gasped, overcome by a surge of shock. What on earth was he saying? And why had he brought a gas can into her house?

Before she could speak, Travis lunged at her. He pushed her against the wall, his wrist pressed against her throat, making her gag. "I don't have a lot of time here, Sarah, so please, don't make this harder for either one of us." His voice came in ragged pants. "I just want my daughter."

"Your daughter?" she choked out. "Lucy's mine, Travis. I adopted her—"

"Because that whore gave her away!" he boomed. "She never even told me that I had a child! If I'd known, I never would have approved a damn adoption!"

Sarah tried to squirm out of his grip, but he held her against the wall, his face hard. "Teresa never gave me a choice," he hissed. "But I have a choice now, and I choose to be a father to my child."

She couldn't believe she was hearing this. Travis had been involved with Teresa? *Travis* was Lucy's father?

And then an even more terrifying thought occurred to her.

"You killed her," she gasped.

Regret flickered in his gaze. "That was a mistake."

Sarah gaped at him. "You *mistakenly* shot her in the heart?"

"I only brought the gun to show her that I meant business, to scare her into telling me what she did with our daughter. I gave her a chance to make amends, to tell me where Lucy was, but she just stood there and gloated about giving our child away. So I shot her."

The Travis she knew no longer seemed to exist. The grief and rage ravaging his normally pleasant face had transformed him into a stranger. She could picture the encounter he had described, perfectly envision Teresa taunting this man, the way she'd taunted everyone else. Despite the fear coursing through her body, Sarah actually experienced a spark of sympathy. Travis had lost his wife and two young sons a year before he moved to Serenade. Finding out he had a daughter, only to discover that the child had been given away without his consent…it must have crushed him, as badly as he'd been crushed when he lost his family in that fire.

Fire.

Her gaze dropped to the gas can. Oh, God. Was he planning on setting her house on fire? With her and Lucy inside it?

No, he wanted Lucy. He'd said so himself.

As if her ears were burning, Lucy's soft cry crackled from the baby monitor, causing both Sarah and Travis to look at it.

"Is that her?" His voice caught in his throat. "Is that my daughter?"

"She's *my* daughter," Sarah said softly.

His eyes blazed. "No! Nobody else is going to take her away from me, not even you, Sarah. Valerie and I had an arrangement, we would raise the baby together, but now that Valerie is out of the picture—"

Sarah gasped in interruption. "What?"

"She was going to tell the cops about my involvement in the kidnapping," Travis said defensively. "I couldn't let that happen."

"You were working together?" Sarah shook the cobwebs from her head. "Valerie joined forces with you even knowing you killed her sister?"

"She didn't know. Nobody knew. But now you do, and I'm sure the good sheriff has figured it out, too." He grabbed her by the collar and yanked her away from the wall. To her terror, he sloshed the gas can from side to side, dousing the walls and floor with gasoline as he pushed her toward the stairs.

Adrenaline spiked in her blood. He wasn't even armed, save for that metal can. She sidestepped, heart pounding. She had to make a run for it, race upstairs to get her baby before—

Pain crashed into the side of her face, making stars dance in front of her eyes.

"Don't even think about it," Travis snapped. "I'll knock you out and leave you in a puddle of gasoline if you try to escape. Now go up the stairs."

She should still fight. Kick him in the crotch, try to get to Lucy. But Travis was a tall man, stronger than her, and his threat of knocking her unconscious refused to leave her head. As long as she cooperated, he wouldn't hurt her. Not until he had Lucy, anyway. She didn't think he'd set fire to the place until he was out of the house, but she was scared he might panic if she fought him, and kill them all.

Taking a breath, Sarah slowly ascended the stairs, shooting Travis a sidelong look. "You framed me for the murder."

His voice was thick with remorse. "I had to. I tried pinning it on Donovan, but it didn't work. When you told me about the threat you made to Teresa, I figured I could use that."

"To cover up the fact that you're a killer?" she said darkly.

"I'm a *father*," he snapped back. "*I'm* the victim here. That bitch thought she could rob me of my child, even after I told her about the agony of losing my family. She deserved to die for what she did."

"And what about me?" she whispered. "Do I deserve to die?"

They reached the top of the stairs.

"No, you don't," he admitted. "But it's the only way."

"It doesn't have to be," she protested. "What if I let you see her? We could work out a visitation sched—"

"*Let* me see her?" he echoed in anger. "She's mine,

Sarah. Not yours. She was never yours. Now where is the nursery?"

She was going to lie, point in the other direction of the hall, but then Lucy started to wail, pretty much announcing her location. Travis gripped Sarah's arm and dragged her down the hall. She thought he would take her to the nursery, but then there was a blur of movement, and the next thing she knew, he was shoving her into the small bathroom across from the baby's room. Her butt landed on the tiled floor with a thump. She registered what had happened just as the door slammed.

Sarah launched herself at it, twisting the knob, but it didn't budge. There was a scraping noise, as if someone was dragging something across the floor. He was barricading the door, trapping her inside.

"Travis!" she screamed, pounding her fists on the door. "Let me out! Please, don't do this!"

There was no reply, only the muffled sound of Lucy's screams. Sarah darted to the bathtub, inhaled deeply, then took off at the door and slammed her shoulder into it. Pain streaked up and down her arm, but the door didn't move.

She couldn't hear Lucy crying anymore.

She kept throwing herself at the door, trying to break it open, but Travis had effectively locked her in. Fear pummeled at her, slapping her skin and bringing tears to her eyes.

"Travis! Don't *do* this!"

Her pleas went unanswered. She couldn't hear a damn thing behind the door. Not footsteps. Not Lucy. Nothing.

And then she smelled the smoke.

Chapter 16

Finn couldn't believe his eyes when the Jeep skidded to a stop in Sarah's driveway.

The house was on fire.

Feeling as though he'd been punched in the gut, he stared in horror at the orange flames licking at the curtains on the second floor. Smoke curled through the open windows, thick gray plumes rising up and getting carried away by the afternoon breeze. The smell of scorched wood drifted toward him, burning his nostrils as his passenger let out a piercing expletive.

"What the hell is going on?" Parsons demanded, opening the door handle and jumping from the vehicle.

Finn dove after him, stunned by what he was seeing. His shock reached a new high when he spotted the silver Lexus parked a few yards away on the dirt. He'd been so focused on the smoke and flames that he'd failed to notice the car. It wasn't Sarah's—she kept her station wagon in the garage.

Bennett.

"He's here," Finn burst out, already pulling his cell phone from his pocket. He tossed it to Parsons, who caught it in surprise. "Speed dial six," he barked. "Volunteer fire chief. Get him over here now!"

As his pulse drummed in his ears, he tore toward the porch, reaching the front door just as it swung open.

Travis Bennett stood in the doorway, his brown eyes wild, his arms clutching a confused Lucy, who let out a cry when she noticed Finn standing there.

Bennett blinked like a deer caught in headlights, then whirled around and ran back into the house. Finn lunged at the door but Bennett had locked it.

"Travis!" he shouted. "Open the door!"

He heard a muffled sound from inside, followed by Lucy's hearty wails. As adrenaline sizzled in his blood, Finn glanced over at Parsons, who had just hung up the phone. "Back door!" he ordered. "He might make a run for it!"

Parsons sprinted off without a word, removing his Glock from his holster as he disappeared around the side of the house. As the odor of smoke grew stronger, thicker, Finn went to work on the door, slamming his shoulders into it. He felt the lock give away and kicked open the door, bursting into the front hall. Smoke instantly filled his nostrils, making his eyes water like a leaky faucet. He coughed, covered his nose with his sleeve, then rushed down the hallway, following the sound of Lucy's cries.

The kitchen. Bennett was in the kitchen. But where was Sarah? He called her name, but there was no answer. The main floor of the house didn't seem to be ablaze. There was a canopy of smoke gathering on the ceiling, but he realized the fire must have been ignited upstairs. He registered the sharp scent of gasoline, noticing that the throw rug near the stairs was soaked. Christ, once the flames from above found their way downstairs, the whole place would turn into a raging inferno.

After a second of indecision, he raced to the kitchen, sliding into the room just as Bennett was stumbling to the patio door.

"Travis!" Finn barked. "Don't move."

Bennett ignored him, holding the baby in one arm as he fumbled for the doorknob. He'd just thrown open the door when Parsons appeared on the back lawn, his gun raised in an ominous pose.

Bennett spun around, only to find himself staring at the barrel of another weapon. Finn saw the panic enter the other man's eyes, the way his gaze dropped to the red-faced baby in his arms.

"Travis, there's no way out," Finn said quietly. "Give me the baby."

Bennett's face turned bright scarlet. "This is my daughter, Finnegan! I'm not giving her to you, or anybody else."

Smoke billowed in through the open doorway. Finn blinked rapidly, trying to ease the sting in his eyes, doing his best not to breathe too deeply. The fire upstairs was getting worse. He could feel the temperature rising, the heat bringing beads of sweat to his forehead. Bennett, too, was sweating, profusely, the acrid scent of his fear and desperation mingling with the smoky haze thickening the air.

"If you cared about your daughter, you would give her to Agent Parsons," Finn told the doctor. "The smoke can't be good for the baby. You're a doctor, Travis, you know this."

Bennett's flushed face became ash-white. As a physician, he was more than aware of the risks of smoke inhalation. And the way Lucy was gulping between sobs insured that smoke was finding its way into her tiny lungs.

"Oh, God," Bennett choked out. "Oh, my God, what am I doing?"

Finn didn't want to feel sympathy for this man. He didn't want to empathize with the agony swimming in Bennett's eyes. But he did. In that moment, he realized that Bennett wasn't an evil man. He was just broken.

"What's happening to me?" Bennett whispered. "I'm a doctor. I took an oath to *save* lives, not take them."

Finn stepped closer. "We need to get Lucy out of this house, Travis."

He glanced past Bennett's shoulders and noticed that the cavalry had arrived. Anna, Max and Jamie all stood behind the glass door. Jamie's violet eyes were lined with worry. Finn saw her look up, probably at the flames ravaging the second floor. Her expression went pale. The fire was bad. He could see it on her face.

"I want you to turn around and look outside," Finn said softly. "There's a woman standing there. Jamie Crawford. You knocked her unconscious when you broke into her house and took Lucy."

Tears streamed down the other man's cheeks, though Finn wasn't certain if due to the smoke filling the room, or from sorrow. Slowly, Travis turned and followed Finn's gaze.

"Give Lucy to Jamie," Finn said with patience he didn't feel. God, where the hell was Sarah? Her absence caused foreboding to climb up his spine, but he forced himself to focus on Bennett. "She'll take good care of Lucy, I promise you."

Bennett's large hand covered Lucy's head, as if he were trying to shield the child from the smoke. Glancing back at Finn, he began to cry in earnest. "I didn't want any of this to happen," the man stammered. "I didn't mean to kill her. I just couldn't lose another child. I couldn't do it again."

Finn's throat tightened. "I know. And believe me, I understand. Sarah and I lost a baby, four years ago. It was—" he took a breath, then coughed when he ended up drawing smoke into his chest "—the worst thing that's ever happened to me. I used the tragedy as an excuse to push the one person I cared about away, and I regret that now."

"There's no excuse for what I've done," Travis whispered. "I deserve to be punished. I deserve to be in prison."

"Get your daughter out of the house first. You can worry about everything else later."

Finn was convinced he had him. He saw Bennett's hand move to the doorknob, saw him start to turn it, but then the other man spun around, his eyes wide. "Sarah!" Bennett blurted out. "I locked her upstairs."

A sledgehammer of horror collided with Finn's chest. "You did *what?*"

"I…I j-just wanted my daughter." Moisture stained Bennett's face. "I have to go and save her!"

The man charged forward, but Finn blocked his path, gesturing to the group outside to approach the door. "You take care of Lucy. I'll get Sarah."

As Jamie and Agent Parsons entered the smoke-filled kitchen, Finn hurried off, hearing Jamie's soft encouragement as she gently took the baby from Travis Bennett. He didn't stick around to watch Parsons arrest the doctor—he just thundered out of the room, reaching the bottom of the stairs right as an enormous fiery beam broke apart from the ceiling and crashed onto the floor. Directly obstructing his path.

Sweat dripped down his face, the heat of the flames unbearable. As little orange wisps licked at his shoes, Finn stared in growing terror at the wall of fire between him and his only way to Sarah.

Sarah bent over as another coughing fit racked her body. She couldn't breathe. Couldn't draw a single puff of air into her aching lungs. The sting from the smoke made moisture pour from her eyes like water from a dam. After spending five minutes banging into the door, she'd finally given up, and the only fruits of her labor were bruises and an incredibly sore arm.

She refused to succumb to the panic, but she was starting to think she might actually die in this tiny bathroom. The crack beneath the door seemed to be glowing. It terrified her to think what lay behind the door. Yellow-orange flames, a black tunnel of smoke. At least she could die knowing that Lucy was safe. She was certain Travis had already whisked her daughter out of the house.

Burying her face in her sleeve, she took a breath, then held it. She couldn't decide what would be worse— burning to death, or dying from the smoke inhalation.

Probably the burning to death part. At least with the smoke she would pass out first.

You are not going to die. Think, Sarah!

She peered through the smoke, studying the window over the toilet. It wasn't very big, probably too tight a fit for her, but hell, she had to try *something*.

She stood on the toilet seat, fighting a wave of dizziness. God, she felt like she was going to faint. She could hardly breathe anymore. Had she ever even opened this window before? For all she knew it was welded shut.

She flicked the lock to the side and pushed against the pane, relief soaring through her when the window creaked open. She stuck her head out and gulped fervently, her chest heaving as the fresh air slid into her body. Dizzy again, this time from the rush of oxygen, but then her head began to clear, and she realized in disappointment that the ground below was scarily far away. It was a twenty-foot drop, at least. She'd break her neck if she tried to jump.

Or you might survive...

Sarah looked at the door, swallowing when she spotted the wisps of smoke curling beneath the doorway. And the wood seemed to be...splintering. Oh, God. The white paint was turning black!

Fighting a jolt of panic, she stuck her head out the window again. She couldn't believe how bright it was. The sun was shining and she could even hear the damn birds chirping. Another glance at the door showed the wood was beginning to crack. Taking a breath, she peered outside and shouted, "Help!" at the top of her lungs.

She expected nothing but silence in response, but to her shock, she suddenly heard Finn's voice.

"Sarah?"

And then he was racing around the side of the house, his blue eyes staring at her in terror. "Sarah!" he yelled. "Christ, you don't know how happy I am to see you!"

Relief flooded her body. "Finn! You have to get me out of here!"

"The fire department volunteers will be here in less than ten minutes. Are you all right up there? How bad is the smoke?"

She glanced behind her, fear clamping around her throat when she saw the hungry flames eating at the charred skeleton of the door. The fire crackled, snaking into the bathroom, then licked at the white shower curtains.

"The room is on fire!" she called down to Finn, her heart pounding.

Even from high above, she could see the unhappiness creasing his handsome features. "Then we don't have any time, sweetheart. You're going to have to jump."

Her stomach clenched with fear. "I can't! It's too high."

"Sarah, listen to me. I want you to lower yourself out the window."

"I can't!"

"Yes, you can." Assurance rang from his tone. "You can do it. Just climb out and let yourself hang. When I say the word, let go."

The flames crept closer, causing the flowered wallpaper to peel and burn. Finn was right. She had no choice but to get out of here. Not unless she wanted to kiss her life goodbye.

Ignoring the panicked butterflies taking flight in her stomach, she pulled herself up onto the window ledge, then lowered herself through the tight space, backward. Letting her legs dangle, just as Finn told her to. She refused to look down. Heights had always been her biggest weakness. She didn't even own a ladder, damn it. That's how scared she was of not having her feet touch the ground.

"Now let go," Finn shouted from below.

Let go?

"I'm here," he added. "I'll catch you."

She sucked in a burst of air, feeling light-headed again. Oh, God. What if he missed? What if she tumbled to the ground and smashed her head in? Her chest heaved, tight with fear, and she couldn't help but twist her head so she could look down at Finn.

To her astonishment, his blue eyes shone with calm determination. "Don't be scared." His husky voice drifted up and wrapped around her heart like a warm embrace. "Take that leap of faith, baby. I promise, I'll catch you."

He was talking about more than just this moment. About more than this jump. Sarah's heart pounded. This was it. Crunch time. Decide once and for all whether she was willing to love Finn again.

When did you stop?

The thought flew into her head, making her swallow hard. She hadn't. She *hadn't* stopped loving him. Not for one single second.

Take that leap of faith.

Sarah couldn't help herself. She began to laugh. There she was dangling twenty feet off the ground, while fire ravaged her home, and yet her heart felt so full she feared it might burst. She *loved* Patrick Finnegan.

"Finn...I'm letting go now."

And then she was soaring through the air, sinking, falling. True to his word, Finn caught her. She landed in his strong arms with a thump, her entire body shaking as it came down from the adrenaline high. Rather than set her on her feet, Finn just supported her bottom and shoulders, and pulled her close, his relief trembling through him. As tears slid down her soot-covered face, Sarah wrapped her arms around his neck and clung to him.

"You caught me," she whispered.

He bent down to look in her eyes, and she saw love shining on his face. "Of course I did," he said thickly. "I told you I would."

Disappointment shuddered inside her when he finally put her down, but then his palms were cupping her chin and his mouth came down over hers in a kiss. "I love you, Sarah," he murmured. "I love you so damn much."

She opened her mouth but he placed his index finger against it, his features taut as he rushed on. "And I'm going to give you all the time you need. I should have never pushed you to make a decision. I was just being my usual, bullheaded self, but I see now that it wasn't fair to either one of us. If you want to be with me, it should be your decision, not the result of an ultimatum that I—"

"I love you."

He faltered, his blue eyes filling with shock. "What?"

This time she was the one putting a finger against his lips. "I love you, Finn. I'm not scared to say it anymore."

His throat bobbed as he visibly swallowed. "What are you saying?"

"I'm saying I don't need time." Joy soared up her chest and surrounded her heart. "I'm saying I want to be with you. I want you and me and Lucy to be a family and—Lucy!" she suddenly cried. "Travis—"

"Jamie took her to the hospital in Grayden, to make sure she didn't inhale too much smoke," Finn cut in, a smile lifting his mouth. "Travis gave himself up. Parsons already took him back to the station."

She couldn't bring herself to voice her next words, but she forced them out. "Then...it's over?"

Finn stroked her cheek so tenderly that tears sprung to her eyes. "It's over, sweetheart. Bennett confessed to killing Teresa—the D.A. will have no choice but to drop the charges against you."

With a happy shout, Sarah threw herself into his arms again, basking in the warmth of his embrace, the feel of his lips pressing against the top of her head. She could've stayed there forever, but then the sound of sirens blared in the air and they both turned to see the town's fire truck racing up her driveway. The reminder had her looking at the house, disbelief flooding her body as she stared at the flames engulfing the entire second floor of her home.

"I..." She tipped her head to meet Finn's eyes. "I guess I'll be moving in with you after all."

Regret lined his forehead. "There's no pressure, Sarah. You don't have to do anything you don't feel comfortable with."

"I don't have to," she agreed. "But I *want* to."

Finn's smile lit up his entire face. "Are you sure?"

"I'm more than sure."

Taking his hand, she led him away from the house. Serenade's volunteer firefighters were already springing to action, aiming hoses at the flames and working to control the blazing conflagration. Sarah and Finn kept walking, neither one looking back. When they reached Finn's Jeep, Sarah pressed her body to his and yanked his head down for a soft kiss. There was a fleeting brush of her lips against his, and then she pulled back and said, "Come on, Patrick. Let's go to the hospital and see our daughter."

Raw, all-consuming emotion flooded his gorgeous

blue eyes. He dipped his head to kiss her once more, then took her hand and murmured, "I can't think of anything else I want to do more."

Epilogue

Two Weeks Later

"Are you really okay with Lucy coming along on our honeymoon?"

Sarah fought a pang of distress as she waited for her husband's answer, but when she looked into his eyes, she saw only warmth and sincerity reflecting back at her. "Lucy is part of our family," Finn said thickly. "Of course I want her with us."

She couldn't control the rush of happiness that filled every inch of her body. Shifting her head, she gazed at Cole and Jamie, who were sitting on the wooden steps of Finn's deck, fussing over Lucy. The couple looked absolutely smitten, Jamie fixing the hem of Lucy's filmy white dress, while Cole tickled the baby's tummy and said something that made his fiancée laugh.

"Jamie will be disappointed," she said with a grin.

"She and Cole were hoping to practice being parents. They're planning on having like a hundred babies."

"So am I," Finn said with a grin.

Her heart jammed in her throat as she wondered how she'd gotten so lucky. Finn had been so damn wonderful these past two weeks. With Travis Bennett arrested for the murder of Teresa Donovan, Serenade had returned to its peaceful, crime-free state, leaving Finn plenty of time to lavish Sarah and Lucy with love and attention during the days. And at night… Her cheeks went hot as she thought of all the passionate nights they'd been sharing. The bad boy she'd fallen in love with always made a reappearance in bed.

Her gaze dropped to the simple silver band around the finger of her left hand. Her husband. It had taken them four years to find their way back to each other. She almost wept when she thought of all the wasted time, all the senseless heartache.

Sarah quickly pushed away thoughts of the past. She and Finn were married now, having just exchanged their vows in a quiet, private ceremony in the backyard of their farmhouse. They had the rest of their lives to make up for all the time they'd lost.

"Well, if you want more babies, then we should definitely get a head start in Aruba." Sarah arched a brow. "Making babies is hard work, you know."

Heat flickered in his eyes. "Guess we'll just have to suck it up and muddle through all the…ugh…sex."

Sarah burst out laughing. "Poor Finn. Don't worry, I'll make it painless for you." She swept her gaze over him. "By the way, did I tell you how sexy you look in that suit?"

"Not half as sexy as you look in that dress."

She glanced down at her white empire-waist dress

with the slender black ribbon wrapped around the bodice. She and Jamie had found it in a boutique in the city, and from the appreciation glittering in Finn's blue eyes, she decided the huge price tag had been worth it. She loved the way Finn looked at her. Like she was the most beautiful creature on this planet.

"Seriously, I'm digging the dress," he went on. "It looks good on you." He lifted an eyebrow. "It would look even better on the bedroom floor, though."

Another laugh pealed out of her chest. "That might be the worst pickup line I've ever heard."

"Did it work?"

Hot streaks of awareness sizzled between them. She stared at her husband, at the black jacket stretched over his broad shoulders, the trim fit of his trousers, and a healthy dose of desire found its way into her bloodstream.

Sarah slanted her head. "Right now? No. But say it again in Aruba, after Lucy's fallen asleep, and you might get a different answer," she said with a faint smile.

"I'm counting on it." Flashing her a grin, he took her hand. "Come on, Mrs. Finnegan. Let's say goodbye to our guests."

"What's the rush?" she teased.

His voice was husky as he said, "Just eager to start our life together. Got a problem with that?"

She leaned on her tiptoes and brushed a kiss over his mouth. "Nope, I don't have a single problem with that."

"Good."

Still grinning, he led her across the yard, where their daughter—and their future—awaited.

* * * * *

SUSPENSE

Heartstopping stories of intrigue and mystery—
where true love always triumphs.

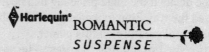

COMING NEXT MONTH
AVAILABLE JANUARY 31, 2012

#1691 HIS DUTY TO PROTECT
Black Jaguar Squadron
Lindsay McKenna

#1692 RANCHER'S PERFECT BABY RESCUE
Perfect, Wyoming
Linda Conrad

#1693 THE PRETENDER
Scandals of Sierra Malone
Kathleen Creighton

#1694 AWOL WITH THE OPERATIVE
Jean Thomas

You can find more information on upcoming Harlequin® titles,
free excerpts and more at www.HarlequinInsideRomance.com.

HRSCNM0112

REQUEST YOUR FREE BOOKS!
2 FREE NOVELS PLUS 2 FREE GIFTS!

ROMANTIC SUSPENSE

Sparked by Danger, Fueled by Passion.

YES! Please send me 2 FREE Harlequin® Romantic Suspense novels and my 2 FREE gifts (gifts are worth about $10). After receiving them, if I don't wish to receive any more books, I can return the shipping statement marked "cancel." If I don't cancel, I will receive 4 brand-new novels every month and be billed just $4.49 per book in the U.S. or $5.24 per book in Canada. That's a saving of at least 14% off the cover price! It's quite a bargain! Shipping and handling is just 50¢ per book in the U.S. and 75¢ per book in Canada.* I understand that accepting the 2 free books and gifts places me under no obligation to buy anything. I can always return a shipment and cancel at any time. Even if I never buy another book, the two free books and gifts are mine to keep forever.

240/340 HDN FEFR

Name	(PLEASE PRINT)	
Address		Apt. #
City	State/Prov.	Zip/Postal Code

Signature (if under 18, a parent or guardian must sign)

Mail to the **Reader Service:**
IN U.S.A.: P.O. Box 1867, Buffalo, NY 14240-1867
IN CANADA: P.O. Box 609, Fort Erie, Ontario L2A 5X3

Not valid for current subscribers to Harlequin Romantic Suspense books.

Want to try two free books from another line?
Call 1-800-873-8635 or visit www.ReaderService.com.

* Terms and prices subject to change without notice. Prices do not include applicable taxes. Sales tax applicable in N.Y. Canadian residents will be charged applicable taxes. Offer not valid in Quebec. This offer is limited to one order per household. All orders subject to credit approval. Credit or debit balances in a customer's account(s) may be offset by any other outstanding balance owed by or to the customer. Please allow 4 to 6 weeks for delivery. Offer available while quantities last.

HRSI1B

Discover a touching new trilogy from
USA TODAY bestselling author

Janice Kay Johnson

Between Love and Duty

As the eldest brother of three, Duncan MacLachlan
is used to being in control and maintaining an
emotional distance; as a police captain it's his job.
But when he meets Jane Brooks, Duncan soon finds
his control slipping away. Together, they fight for a
young boy's future, and soon Duncan finds himself
hoping to build a future with Jane.

Available February 2012

From Father to Son
(March 2012)

The Call of Bravery
(April 2012)

*Louisa Morgan loves being around children.
So when she has the opportunity to tutor bedridden Ellie,
she's determined to bring joy back into the motherless
girl's world. Can she also help Ellie's father open his
heart again? Read on for a sneak peek of*

THE COWBOY FATHER

by Linda Ford,
available February 2012 from Love Inspired Historical.

Why had Louisa thought she could do this job? A bubble of self-pity whispered she was totally useless, but Louisa ignored it. She wasn't useless. She could help Ellie if the child allowed it.

Emmet walked her out, waiting until they were out of earshot to speak. "I sense you and Ellie are not getting along."

"Ellie has lost her freedom. On top of that, everything is new. Familiar things are gone. Her only defense is to exert what little independence she has left. I believe she will soon tire of it and find there are more enjoyable ways to pass the time."

He looked doubtful. Louisa feared he would tell her not to return. But after several seconds' consideration, he sighed heavily. "You're right about one thing. She's lost everything. She can hardly be blamed for feeling out of sorts."

"She hasn't lost everything, though." Her words were quiet, coming from a place full of certainty that Emmet was more than enough for this child. "She has you."

"She'll always have me. As long as I live." He clenched his fists. "And I fully intend to raise her in such a way that even if something happened to me, she would never feel like I was gone. I'd be in her thoughts and in her actions every day."

Peace filled Louisa. "Exactly what my father did."

Their gazes connected, forged a single thought about fathers and daughters...how each needed the other. How sweet the relationship was.

Louisa tipped her head away first. "I'll see you tomorrow."

Emmet nodded. "Until tomorrow then."

She climbed behind the wheel of their automobile and turned toward home. She admired Emmet's devotion to his child. It reminded her of the love her own father had lavished on Louisa and her sisters. Louisa smiled as fond memories of her father filled her thoughts. Ellie was a fortunate child to know such love.

Louisa understands what both father and daughter are going through. Will her compassion help them heal—and form a new family? Find out in
THE COWBOY FATHER
by Linda Ford, available February 14, 2012.

Love Inspired Books celebrates 15 years of inspirational romance in 2012! February puts the spotlight on Love Inspired Historical, with each book celebrating family and the special place it has in our hearts. Be sure to pick up all four Love Inspired Historical stories, available February 14, wherever books are sold.

Harlequin *Presents*

USA TODAY bestselling author

Sarah Morgan

brings readers another enchanting story

ONCE A FERRARA WIFE...

When Laurel Ferrara is summoned back to Sicily
by her estranged husband, billionaire
Cristiano Ferrara, Laurel knows things are about
to heat up. And Cristiano's power is a potent
reminder of his Sicilian dynasty's unbreakable rule:
once a Ferrara wife, always a Ferrara wife....

Sparks fly this February